WOLFISH

TERRY SPEAR

PUBLISHED BY:

Wilde Ink Publishing

Wolf*ish*

Copyright © 2025 by Terry Spear

Cover Copyright by Rainy Day Art

Discover more about Terry Spear at:

http://www.terryspear.com/

Print ISBN: 978-1-63311-120-2

Ebook ISBN: 978-1-63311-200-1

SYNOPSIS

As a wolf opening a gift shop with Halloween décor, a forensic anthropologist, and an author who writes books on old cemeteries, she discovers a skeleton, a month old, in an 18th-century cemetery, and the trouble begins.

Selena Rivers loves working in a wolf-run town and meeting Deputy Sheriff Daniel Hoffman, who assists her at every turn. But when she has to identify skeletons of recently murdered women, he must protect her from those who would harm her and himself. They must learn who the women are and who is responsible for their deaths.

Daniel is all for romancing the wolf, which comes with the added commitment to keep them both safe in this dangerous, mystery adventure. She has never met a wolf like him, and she has every intention of protecting him from the threat, too, and more.

This is another Halloween story for your enjoyment!

To Kendra McEvoy—thanks for all your funny clips about wolves, bears, and other shifter types. They make my day! I appreciated your help, too, when I couldn't locate characters from earlier stories, and you were right there with the names! This book is dedicated to you.

1

Sweating up a storm, Selena Rivers had an appointment with the pack leaders of Silver Town to open a holiday store. She didn't know what the big deal was. She was a wolf; they were wolves. However, she also had to undergo a background check at the sheriff's office and meet with other business owners to ensure she was a good fit.

Sure, she would design her store in the same style as the old western silver mining town, and she was looking forward to it. But she did worry they wouldn't think she was qualified to run a shop. In truth, she had no qualifications whatsoever. Surely others who had started their businesses in Silver Town hadn't either and were doing fine.

One of her reasons for setting up a business there was to write a book about the old Silver Town cemeteries. None of them were documented. This would be her thirteenth book in the series, and she was eager to explore the graveyards after the store was closed for the night.

She arrived at Darien Silver's home and met with him, his wife, Lelandi, the co-leader of the pack, and a licensed psychologist, his second-in-command, Jake Silver, and his third-in-command, Tom Silver, both his brothers. She was surprised to smell that Lelandi was a red wolf. They were much rarer. The Silvers were all gray wolves like her.

For now, she felt she was in the Inquisition.

Lelandi brought cookies and hot chocolate to the sunroom for everyone to enjoy. The sun filled the room with warmth, and a crackling fire in the fireplace cheered things up.

"I'm sorry if this seems like a little bit of overkill." Lelandi sounded like a psychologist. "We just want to ensure we have the best candidates to set up shop here that will be successful. We don't like to see good folks start a business and then lose everything."

"Has that happened often?" Maybe setting up a shop in Silver Town wasn't a good idea. Selena did worry she might fail. She was a trained forensic anthropologist, an author, not a holiday shop owner.

Lelandi nodded. "Twice. We don't want anyone to have high expectations and then for it not to work out."

"Have you had a similar business at a different location?" Darien asked.

"No. But I'm sure I can manage just fine."

"What is your background?" Jake finished off his cocoa and grabbed another pumpkin-shaped sugar cookie.

"Uhm, a forensic anthropologist."

Everyone just stared at her.

Yeah, not excellent credentials for opening a shop.

Then Lelandi smiled. "What an interesting job."

"It has been. Listen, I have the money, and I want to give this a try." She wanted to have an income and a job, though she had considerable investments, so she really didn't need the income while she spent her nights sleuthing at the cemetery.

Besides, after testifying in so many trials based on her forensic findings, she was glad the criminals were prosecuted and most ended up in jail, but three of them were released on bail and went after her. Stalking her, terrorizing her. It didn't matter that she had restraining orders against them. She was glad to leave Fort Wayne, Indiana, and the worry that the men stalking her would turn deadly.

After more questions about her financial credentials, Lelandi signed off on her starting up a shop. Then Darien and his brothers did.

"Thank you. I'm sure it will be a success." Selena hoped.

"I'm sure it will be." Lelandi sounded sure of herself.

However, Selena still had two more appointments before she was cleared to proceed, pending approval from their end. She'd already found the empty shop she wanted to use, but she was afraid it would sell before she could buy it, even though the realtor had told her that it had been vacant for several months now. It was situated between a tea shop and a dress shop, so she figured the traffic from the other shops would help her store get noticed and boost sales.

Next, she went to the Victorian Tea Shop to meet the other business owners. A small brass bell jangled overhead, sending a ripple of a tinkling sound through the entryway as the front door swung inward, announcing her arrival as she stepped inside.

The interior of the Victorian Tea Shop was a dream of romantic Victorian gifts and decorations, with lace doilies covering mahogany tabletops and lace curtains suffused with the buttery light of the sun filtering in. Along each wall, rows of mismatched plates—delicate bone china, some with hairline cracks spidery across their surfaces—caught the glow and threw it back in soft, iridescent fragments.

Mahogany shelves, scarred by decades of use, groaned under the collective weight of teapots in every conceivable form, from silver-plated to floral and Chinese styled. All decorated with Victorian-era lace, hot chocolate pitchers, old-time pictures, and Victorian metal signs, the Victorian Tea Shop was charming.

The sweet, fruity, and floral aromas of tea, spicy soups, and grilled sandwiches filled the air, making her stomach growl.

A dark-haired woman came out of a back room, dressed in high-heeled boots, a short plaid skirt in orange and moss green, and an orange sweater. She greeted Selena with a big smile. "Come in, sugar. We're back here. I'm Silva, and I'm the proprietor of the tea shop. Wait, let me get your complimentary order for something to drink and a slice of pie or cake." She handed her a menu.

All the other ladies there had placed their orders so Selena perused the menu. "Oh, everything looks good. In the spirit of fall and Halloween, I'll get the Witches Brew Cider Spices Wassail and apple-cinnamon cheesecake."

"My mate and I also own the Silver Town Tavern, a short distance away," Silva said, as she delivered the cheesecake and wassail to Selena. "These are the MacTire sisters, Laurel, Ellie, and Meghan, though they have since mated and taken their mates' names, but we still think of them fondly this way. You've probably met them since they own the Victorian Silver Town Hotel where you're staying."

"Yes, of course," Selena said, greeting them. She liked seeing friendly, familiar faces. She relaxed while she drank her wassail and took a bite of her cheesecake.

"We're glad to see you want to open up a gift shop here," the triplets said in unison with a distinctive Irish burr.

"We wanted to be part of this process," Laurel said.

Selena loved how welcoming everyone was.

"I'm Kayla Wolff, and this is my sister, Roxie. My brothers, Blake and Landon, my sister, and I own the ski lodge, and we have our own gift shop. But it mostly caters to skiers."

"I'm Bertha Hastings, and I own Hastings Bed and Breakfast. I don't really sell gifts, but I wanted to meet our new business owner." She was an older woman, wearing a flowery dress in fall colors, and all smiles.

"I'm Maxine Fox, the cat lady. I only have two, mind you, but it has still become my nickname. I own the dress shop a couple of doors down. I carry mostly clothes."

"I'm Faye, and my husband, Roger Boatman, and I own the Silver Town Theater. We sell mostly movie-related gifts, but I wanted to meet you too."

"That's me as far as selling tea-related merchandise," Silva said. "And the tavern only sells food and drink. So what experience do you have in running a shop?" Silva asked. Before Selena could say none, Silva continued. "I worked for my mate at his tavern until I set up the Victorian Tea Shop."

"It's lovely," Selena said, trying not to appear conscientious about not having run a shop before.

"We had run a family lodge for years before we came here," Kayla Wolff said.

"We had been buying and selling small Victorian hotels for years before we settled here," Meghan MacTire said.

"I've run my bed and breakfast for eons," Bertha said.

"I sold my beachwear shop in Florida and settled down here, changing the clothes I sell for each season and special occasions, like tuxes for New Year's Eve. I still have a market for beachwear for visitors staying at the Wolff lodge, which has a swimming pool. You wouldn't believe how many people forget to pack a bathing suit for a winter ski trip," Maxine said.

"Oh, I've done that," Selena said.

"Yeah, me too," Kayla said.

"We ran a movie theater in Indiana before we moved here. We were glad to be around other wolves," Faye said.

"The same with us," the MacTire sisters said.

Laurel said, "We were flipping beautiful, small Victorian hotels and enjoyed doing it, but once we arrived in Silver Town, we were here to stay."

"I, well, I haven't had any experience running a shop, but it's something I really have my heart set on." Selena figured she wouldn't have any issues with people threatening her while running a gift shop in Silver Town like she had when she was testifying at court on her forensic cases.

"Well, let me tell you, sugar, we're all here to assist you. With our combined experiences and the wolves in Silver Town to support new businesses, we're all here to help make your dream come true," Silva said.

Everyone agreed, and Selena felt a modicum of relief as long as the sheriff's department didn't have an issue with a background check that showed she wasn't qualified to do the job.

"Oh, what do you intend to call the shop?" Laurel asked.

"The Howling Wolf."

"I love it," Ellie said.

"Yes, you'll fit right in," Roxie Wolff said.

"A perfect name for a shop in a wolf-run town. What merchandise do you plan to carry?" Meghan asked.

"Holiday and special occasions wearables and gifts. So fall and Halloween merchandise for now. And winter items, Christmas, then spring, Easter, and a patriotic theme. Summer holidays. Just a change of seasons kind of shop."

"Where are you going to set up shop?" Silva asked.

"Between your tea shop and Maxine's clothes store."

Silva brightened. "Perfect. An empty shop always makes it seem like stores are failing. That will provide more traffic to all our stores on Main Street."

"What happened to the two businesses that didn't make it?" Selena asked.

"Oh," Laurel said, "in both cases, the owners were disagreeable wolves. Word quickly spread, and no one would do business with them. One was a used-and-new bookstore owner, but he only wanted to sell classic fiction and rare books. We didn't know this at the time. We were excited to see that he would carry all kinds of different books to read. Most of us wanted to read romance, historical fiction, paranormal fiction, thrillers, mysteries, and westerns. And the kids wanted children's books. He refused to carry anything we were interested in reading and was quickly out of business."

"Wow, unreal." Selena couldn't imagine a store not carrying merchandise that customers wanted to buy.

"The other store that failed in town copied what everyone else was doing, offering to sell the same merchandise we were all carrying," Silva said. "We try to have unique gifts so that shoppers will have a variety of items to choose from. If you go into one store and they carry the same as all the other stores, that hurts sales. We all talked to the store owner, but she wouldn't go along with the plan. All the wolves in the pack boycotted her."

"I'll keep that in mind. Do I need to check in with you all?" Selena sure didn't want to step on toes when she opened her new business.

"It wouldn't hurt. We all do that with each other when we want to buy something that might be sold by the other stores. Of course, sometimes we do have some duplicate items, but most of our items for sale are unique to our shop," Silva said. "For instance, I sell teacups, and tea-related signage, statues, books on teas, and teas. No one else does."

"At the theater, we sell movie posters and everything movie-related," Faye said. "So we don't compete with anyone."

"For us at the Timberline Ski Lodge, our merchandise is ski-related," Roxie said. "So we don't have any problem with anyone there."

"We'll sign off on you opening your new shop. As soon as you're ready to set it up, let us know, and we'll be there to help," Laurel said, her sisters agreeing.

Selena smiled. For the first time since she had started this venture, she was hopeful this was going to work out.

She thanked the ladies and Silva for the wassail and cheese-cake, which were out of this world. Afterward, she headed to the sheriff's department. Surely they couldn't thwart her when the business owners and the pack leaders had already signed off.

When she arrived at the office, the sheriff and two of his deputies were out on a call. She shouldn't have been annoyed. That was their duty, but she wanted to get this done. But then another deputy came out of an office to speak with her.

"Hello, I'm Deputy Sheriff Daniel Hoffman." He greeted her with a smile and a warm handshake.

"I guess you know I'm Selena Rivers."

"Selena, goddess of the moon. Radiant and enchanting," he said.

She smiled. "Not too many people know that."

"I did my research."

He was dark-haired and eyed, having a chiseled face; his hair was cut just a little longer than military regulation, which made her wonder if he had a prior military background. She had a thing for men in uniform, especially when they were wolves. "The sheriff told me to investigate your background. Come, have a seat in my office."

She took a seat across from his desk while he sat on the edge of it, intimidating, towering over her.

"So why did you come here to Silver Town?"

"I write books about cemeteries," she blurted out, figuring he would guess her setting up a shop wasn't all she was up to.

He raised his brows, smiling a little. "I thought you were opening a shop."

"I am, and I am writing a book on the side. The cemeteries are old, dating back to the eighteenth century, and I photograph them.

When my shop is closed for the night, I'll be documenting details about the ones around Silver Town."

"We have several. They're not mapped. I can show you where they are."

"Thank you. That would be appreciated." It sounded like he was going to approve her application to own a business here. She couldn't be more thrilled.

"So you're a forensic anthropologist by trade."

"Yes. I study remains."

"For law enforcement?"

She suspected he'd done a comprehensive background check on her already. "Yes, but I needed a change of pace." And to get away from her stalkers.

"I don't blame you. Will you be digging up *our* skeletons?"

"Do you have any in your family tree?"

Daniel laughed. "Don't we all?"

"For sure." She liked his sense of humor. "If I find some human bones unearthed, I'll study them."

"And you're single?"

The question took her aback. "Well, yes. Are you?"

He smiled. "Sure am. Okay, you're approved. Good luck with your venture. If you need any help with the shop, ask. And when you're ready to look up the cemeteries, I'm only a call away." He handed her a business card.

"I don't need the sheriff to sign off?"

"No, he said I could do it."

"All right, well, I'm thrilled. Thanks so much." She shook Daniel's hand, who shook hers warmly and a little longer than she thought necessary, making her smile, and he released her hand.

Then she hurried out of the office to purchase the store. Once she was at the real estate office, she met with Regina Fairhaven, the woman she had spoken to before. "I've been approved to open a shop next to the tea shop, and I'm ready to purchase the store."

Selena had already negotiated a good deal for it because it had been sitting idle for so many months. "What had it been before this?"

"A rare bookstore."

"Oh." That disagreeable owner who wouldn't carry the kind of books the townspeople wanted to read. A surefire way to go out of business. No wonder Silva wanted her to open another shop in its place.

"You might have heard that the previous owner had been boycotted. I'm sure you will have the opposite experience."

Selena sure hoped so. Then she signed the paperwork, paid for the shop, and headed over to it with the keys in hand. For the first time since starting this venture, she knew this was becoming a reality, now that she was no longer apprehensive about getting so many people's approval.

She walked inside and stared at the four walls. A lovely, oak display window would showcase her merchandise, and an oak counter would be used to sell merchandise. She would also hire a couple of clerks if she received a large volume of business so she could take breaks if she needed to.

For now, she needed stands for clothes and shelving, and then she would work with the other businesses to determine which merchandise she could sell that didn't compete with theirs. It appeared that the previous owner must have had portable shelving and either took it with him or sold it.

The movie theater, Hastings Bed and Breakfast, and the MacTire sisters' hotel wouldn't be a problem. Maxine Fox's clothes shop could be more of an issue. Selena wouldn't order anything tea-related, which was in Silva's tea shop, so that wasn't any big deal either. The Timberline Ski Lodge's gift shop shouldn't be a problem if she didn't carry ski-related merchandise.

She decided on all-wooden shelves for the old-western town appeal. No chrome clothing racks. The counter was a perfect fit.

Behind the counter, she would put a long mirror to make the store appear even larger. She was glad the shop had a restroom, something she knew would be important when it opened.

Then she called Silva as a courtesy, but also because she was dying to tell her since she had been so welcoming. "I bought the shop."

"I'm so excited for you. What do you need first?"

"A carpenter to put in wooden shelves."

"Frank Sutter can do the job." Silva gave her his phone number.

Selena was so glad she had asked Silva for advice. Within the hour, Frank came over to learn what she wanted, took measurements, and suggested trimming the shelves with decorative molding to give them a more antiquated, charming appeal.

She loved his suggestions, and he quickly began to work on it. "Can you add a mirror behind the counter?"

"Framed?"

"Yes."

"Sure can. Do you need dressing rooms?"

"Oh yes, two please." Boy, did she luck out. She hadn't even thought of that, though if anyone wanted to try on sweaters, sweatshirts, or T-shirts, they could.

In the middle of all the chaos, Deputy Sheriff Daniel Hoffman walked in. "I heard you were making a lot of noise over here."

"Is that against the city ordinances?" She really thought the neighboring stores had complained about the noise Frank was making, and already she was in trouble.

"I dropped by to check and see if you need my help with anything."

Her whole expression brightened. "Are you off for the rest of the day?" Selena asked, surprised.

"I've been given the job to make sure you have everything you need."

"Good. You can help me set up these shelves," Frank said.

Daniel smiled at Selena and removed his shirt, showing off some hot muscles. "I don't want to get my uniform dirty."

Right. She asked about clothes carousels, in case Frank could make them, which he said he would.

"I can have them done tomorrow."

"Oh, that would be great."

A mirror arrived to be placed behind the counter, but he would have to add the frame. The shelves were installed, and he began staining them.

By the time the men finished staining the shelves, Frank had stains all over his painter's bib overalls, while Daniel had stains on his arms and chest, as if he had gotten a filtered suntan.

"See what I mean? I don't have any stains on my uniform."

Now she understood what he was getting at, and he hadn't removed his shirt to just show off his beautiful abs.

"Turpentine's in that box," Frank said. "I'll be back tomorrow to frame and install the mirror, set up the clothes racks, and build the changing rooms." Then he left.

Poor Daniel was muddling through it while trying to wipe off all the stains.

She said, "Here, let me do it." At this rate, she would never get out of the shop tonight if she didn't assist him.

"Thanks."

"If you miss a spot, it'll get on your uniform," she explained, then felt foolish for having mentioned it.

"Of course, I appreciate it."

Once he washed up in the restroom, she thanked him for helping out. "I would call that going above and beyond the call of duty."

"I'm glad to assist. How about dinner? At the Silver Town Tavern?" He came out of the restroom, drying himself.

He was so hot. "And drinks?" She could use a drink.

"Yep. I'll go home and change, and then I'll pick you up at the Silver Town Hotel in an hour."

"Okay, sounds good. And then we could maybe go to one of the cemeteries afterward."

Just the smile he gave her made her believe he hadn't thought they would end the date with a visit to a cemetery. She hoped he didn't mind.

2

Daniel never thought his boss would be into matchmaking. But as soon as Sheriff Peter Jorgenson learned Selena was applying to have a shop in town and that she was a single gray wolf who needed a background check, Peter made sure Daniel had the first chance to meet her.

That meant giving him a few days off once Daniel said the wolf was intriguing so he could help her set up her store. The rest of her idea—him taking her to cemeteries at night, not something he would typically think of for a date night, but at least she was recep tive to dinner. He had every intention of taking her to lunch tomorrow also, if she was agreeable.

When a new she-wolf was in town, many bachelor males would be interested, and he had to show he was totally intrigued by her right off the bat. A pretty brunette with amber eyes? A forensic anthropologist who worked with law enforcement piqued his inter- est. He could imagine all the tales she could tell.

He headed home and hurried to dress in something nice, his favorite fall sweater, a pair of blue jeans, and cowboy boots. He grabbed a jacket and hoped he wouldn't arrive too early at the Silver Town Hotel to pick Selena up.

AT THE HOTEL, all the sisters greeted Selena, eager to hear how the shop was going. "Frank did such a wonderful job on the shelving. Even Daniel Hoffman came by to help."

"Daniel did?" Laurel asked, a sparkle in her eyes.

"Yeah. The sheriff gave him some time off to assist me."

The ladies shared conspiratorial looks and smiled.

"We just have a few things left to do, and I'm going to start ordering merchandise—fall, Halloween. I'll have a large red, howling wolf and a black one in the front window for fall and Halloween. For winter, I'll change it out to a white one. New Year's Eve, I'll have the white and black ones on display. A gray howling wolf will be out there for the rest of the year."

"That sounds lovely," Ellie said.

"I love how your store title is the Howling Wolf and your theme will be too," Meghan said. "It suits our wolf community."

"I do too," Laurel said. "If you need any assistance with decorating your shop, just let us know and we'll help. We've already done all our fall decorating."

"That would be great," Selena said. "You've done a lovely job with yours." Fall flowers and leaf garlands wrapped around the banister going up the stairs to the guest rooms on the second floor of their Victorian hotel, and across their counter. They had a lovely fall wreath on the door. Bouquets were located throughout the lobby. "For now, I just need to change my clothes to get ready for my date. What is the dress code for the tavern?"

"None really," Meghan said. "Some dress up and others dress down. Wear what you feel like for the occasion."

"Okay, thanks."

"It's a good thing that you're not going alone. All the bachelor wolves would be trying to buy your drinks," Ellie said.

Selena laughed. "No, Daniel is taking me."

"Ha!" Laurel said. "He's already staking his claim. The other wolves will be disappointed."

Selena had never been to a wolf-run town, where the bachelor wolves would be flocking to get her attention. She was amused.

Once she was in her room, she dressed in a wool plaid skirt in pumpkin-and-olive green, a pumpkin sweater to match, and high-heeled boots. She grabbed a jacket and headed for the lobby.

She sat on one of the sofas in the lobby and began ordering items for her shop. She'd already found just the howling wolves she'd wanted, all hand-carved wood but stained or painted to simulate white, black, red, and gray wolves.

Then Daniel arrived ten minutes early to pick her up. She liked it when a date was early.

"You look lovely." Daniel escorted her to his vehicle.

"So do you." He was dressed in a pumpkin-orange sweater that was similar to hers, so it looked like they had dressed to match, which she thought was cute. His blue jeans and cowboy boots were charming. Dressy casual.

The last guy she dated, who had been in law enforcement, didn't know how to dress once he wasn't wearing a uniform.

Going out with a nicely dressed man made her feel special.

They drove over to the tavern, where the lights lit up the inside and outside of the building, which made it look festive. A few hardy males were seated outside in the chilly temperature.

She was worried the tavern would be packed, and they would have to wait for a long time to find a table. But when they walked inside, Silva greeted them with a big smile. "Your table is right this way." She motioned in the direction.

They actually had a table just for two by the big windows, which made it really special.

"I made a reservation earlier to make sure we had a table for dinner," Daniel said.

He got Brownie points for that too.

"Your place is charming," she told Silva as she dropped off menus and water for them.

"Thanks. I decorated it myself. Sam, my mate, isn't interested in that sort of thing, though he hangs the lights I ask him to and anything else I need done."

That made her mate a hero, Selena was thinking.

The tavern was decorated with fall flowers and pumpkins, not for sale, but purely decorative. No competition for her merchandise here.

"What can I get you to drink?"

"This pumpkin spice drink looks good," Selena said.

"I'll have the same," Daniel said.

She liked that he was joining her for a cocktail. Her last boyfriend always drank beer and didn't care for wine, cocktails, or even champagne.

"So what do you do, other than keep the peace and help Frank build shelves and the like for new shopkeepers?"

"I love to ski and hike. I even do a little bit of gardening in the spring—some herbs, tomatoes, and onions. It's just me, so I don't need a lot."

"But you cook, or you wouldn't need to grow anything to eat."

He smiled. "Yeah, I love to cook."

"I like the same kind of things. I love cooking too. I'm not a great skier, but I can manage the intermediate slopes."

"Living here, you'll end up on the advanced slopes, guaranteed, once the slopes are open."

If she had time. She imagined that with her research at night and taking care of the shop during the day, she wouldn't have much spare time to go skiing.

"Will you hire additional staff to help you out at the store?"

"Once it gets busy."

Silva returned with their drinks. "Have you decided on what you want to order, or do you need more time?"

"Oh, I would love the prime rib, mashed potatoes, and broccoli," Selena said.

"I'll have the prime rib, a baked potato, and spinach," Daniel said.

"I'll bring them right out."

"Do Darien and Lelandi and his brothers and their mates often eat here?" Selena asked Silva before she placed the order.

"Yeah. The table in the back is reserved for them." Silva pointed to the table. "No one eats there unless they are a special guest. Mostly their cousins and their mates also eat at that table in the corner."

"So they have a large extended family."

Silva nodded. "They do."

Just then, three rowdy men entered the tavern. They'd been drinking alcohol by the looks of it as they stumbled into the entryway.

Daniel stood up from the table, stalked toward the entryway, and stopped them at the entrance from going any further. "You have to have reservations to eat here." He handed them a business card for the tavern. "You can call this number."

"Hey, come on, man. They threw us out of the ski lodge restaurant, and we're hungry," one of the men said.

They were big, bearded guys, and Selena didn't believe Daniel could manage the three men on his own.

Suddenly, Sam was there with Daniel. He was the size of a grizzly bear, black-bearded, black-haired, eyes narrowed. "I own the Silver Town Tavern, and that's the rules."

"Look, there's an open table over there," one of the other men said.

"It's reserved," Sam said.

Jake and Tom Silver joined them at the door. "Do as Sam said. Make a reservation or get something to eat out of town," Jake said.

Several other men were eyeing the newcomers, looking like

they were ready to use some muscle if the party of three didn't leave.

The three finally stomped off, throwing the business card Daniel had given them onto the floor. He picked it up and pocketed it.

When he rejoined Selena, she was sipping on her drink. "That was impressive. Is that table really reserved?"

"It has a card on it. But even if it wasn't, this is an establishment that doesn't cater to humans. Only shifters are allowed. First, it was only for wolves, but then we had an unexpected visit from jaguars. Since then, a grizzly bear couple from Minnesota, and two couples on vacation from Yuma Town—cougar shifters—have visited. So it's become an exclusive shifter establishment, but predominantly wolves eat and drink here."

"Cougars and jaguars? Never met any."

"But you've met bears?"

"In Minnesota. I wonder if I had met the bear couple who visited here."

"I never knew their names. Everyone's been super friendly, just like we have been to them. I wouldn't be surprised if some of their kind might end up settling here someday," Daniel said.

"They'll be welcome?"

"As long as they follow our pack rules. I've heard the polars bears have a governing council that rules over the sleuth of bears. The jaguars and cougars are on their own, so they would all have to learn to take direction from wolves."

"Fascinating." She hoped she would meet some of them while she lived here.

"So you want me to take you to one of the cemeteries tonight still?"

"Yeah, I would like to do that after dinner, if it's not too inconvenient for you."

"Sure, we can do that."

Then she thought about the men making reservations at the restaurant. "You gave the men the tavern's business card. What if the men had made a reservation?"

"Sam tells them they're booked solid for months, and they can't make a reservation for too many months into the future. That card is for humans only."

She laughed.

"We have to have some place that's just for us," he said.

"I don't blame you. It's nice to be able to talk about shifter issues without worrying about humans overhearing us."

"Exactly."

Then their food was served, and she swore she'd never had prime rib this good. It was medium rare and delightfully tender.

The Silvers all stopped by their table and introduced Jake's mate, Alicia, and Tom's mate, Elizabeth, to her and welcomed Selena to the pack.

She hadn't ever belonged to a pack and hadn't considered that. Even though Daniel had told her other shifters would have to obey the pack leaders, which would mean she would belong to the pack, too. But she loved how welcoming everyone was.

A few bachelor males on the way out of the tavern also stopped by their table and introduced themselves. Did they believe she might be interested in one of them if she decided she didn't care for Daniel's company any longer?

She was afraid Daniel would be offended, but he just smiled at the guys as if they were too late in the game. She appreciated that he was good-natured about it. Her last boyfriend wouldn't have been.

When her boyfriend was coming back from the men's room at a club last year, and a random guy had asked her to dance, her boyfriend had been furious with the guy and with her for being hit on like it had been her fault! That had been the living end of it for her, and she'd broken up with the wolf.

After Daniel approved her application for the shop, helped Frank set up the shelves, and said he would help with the rest of the work tomorrow, she really thought the world of him. But he also took her out to dinner and would show her a cemetery afterward, so the other men had missed out.

Though things could change if Selena and Daniel decided after a few dates that they genuinely weren't suited to each other.

When they were done eating, Daniel drove her back to the hotel so she could change into something she could wear to walk through the cemetery.

She didn't imagine that any of his previous dates had wanted to see a cemetery to finish off the night.

As soon as she returned to the lobby where he was waiting for her, they left.

They finally reached the graveyard near one of the closed silver mines. He explained, "This is the oldest one we have so I thought you might like to see it first."

"Oh, yes, perfect." She started to explore the graveyard where the silver miners of the 1700s now rested beneath weathered stones, while he used his flashlight to illuminate them. Though as wolves, they could still see well at night.

NEVER IN HIS wildest dreams had Daniel envisioned taking a date after a delightful dinner to a cemetery to explore it. Though he'd never imagined meeting a new she-wolf in town, or that he would hit it off with her right away. He thought she felt the same way. The other guys had amused him by trying to make her acquaintance at the tavern.

He just had to make sure he didn't let down his guard, and he continued to date her. He watched her as she crouched down to touch a graveyard stone with reverence. She intrigued him like no other wolf he'd ever met. Some of it was that she had worked with law enforcement before. When she'd met the other bachelor males, she'd appeared amused but not interested. He appreciated that.

He continued to follow her as she wound her way around the dilapidated headstones. Some were so worn that no one could read the inscriptions. Others were only partially readable.

"Here's one!" she said, enthusiasm evident, and took a picture.

He thought she'd found an exposed skeleton and hurried to join her. But it was only a headstone, with the full name intact.

"I can research him. Let's go home now. Sometimes I find lots of names I can investigate," she said, as they headed back to his vehicle. "Sometimes I don't find any. Even finding only one in this old cemetery is a real boon. Though I would love to look further and find more, it's getting late."

At least he didn't have to work his regular job tomorrow, but knowing Frank, he would be up early to work all day and finish the last projects for her shop.

Back at the hotel, she leaned in, her lips grazing his cheek, and she wrapped her arms around him. Daniel returned the embrace, a smile warming his face. The cemetery discovery had meant more to her than he'd anticipated—he could feel it in the way she held on just a bit longer. Showing her the graveyard tonight had been exactly the right move.

"Until morning," she murmured, already turning toward the staircase.

Hell, he felt like a million bucks. Then he left the hotel and headed home, thinking of the possibilities with her, though he shouldn't get ahead of himself. He knew the locations of two more old cemeteries, but he would canvass the residents to see if they were aware of any others.

Who would ever have thought he would be interested in cemeteries? Well, he wasn't as much as he was intrigued with the goddess of the moon.

3

The next morning, Daniel dropped by the hotel to pick up the shop keys from Selena so he and Frank could get started on the remaining projects. He'd brought kolaches for breakfast.

"Oh, wow. Thanks. I can grab us something to drink from Silva's shop," Selena said, giving him a kiss and hug.

He wrapped his arms around her and gave her a warm embrace. "That would be perfect. She'll be open about the time we get started."

Selena loved how affectionate he was.

He drove her to the shop, and she loved how all the shops down Main Street had awnings over the sidewalk. She knew just what she was going to hang on hers. One large skeleton would be climbing the pole for the awning, and another would be sitting atop the awning with his legs dangling over the edge.

"I didn't know you would be ready this early," she said.

"Frank wants to get your store set up today."

"Oh, that's good. I've been ordering merchandise."

"Let me know if you need any help with it. What are you going to do about a place to stay?"

"I've thought of getting an apartment I can rent monthly that I can try out. Then after that, I'll look for a house to buy." Once they arrived at the shop, she asked what they wanted to drink.

Frank said, "I brought a thermos of coffee from home."

"You, Daniel?"

"Pumpkin spice cold brew."

She smiled. "My favorite too." Then she headed over to the tea shop.

SILVA GREETED Selena when she arrived. Selena smiled. "I feel any place I go, you'll be there to greet me."

Silva smiled. "What do you want to drink and eat?"

"Just two pumpkin spice cold brews."

"Two. One wouldn't be for Deputy Sheriff Daniel Hoffman, would it?"

"Yes, he's helping Frank build more things in the shop."

"Sheriff Jorgenson gave him the time off?" Silva asked.

"Yes. Wasn't that nice of him?"

Silva chuckled. "Peter's mated to Meghan MacTire. It sounds to me like she and her sisters are doing a bit of matchmaking without even telling me."

Selena laughed. "Well, we're enjoying each other's company. See you later." She took the drinks back over to her shop and thought how much fun it would be to get a special drink from the tea shop to start her daily routine.

"Here you go," she told Daniel as she entered her shop.

They enjoyed their kolaches and drinks, and then the guys went to work while she ordered more merchandise.

Halfway through the day, Daniel took Selena to Silva's shop to have lunch. Frank had brought his lunch from home.

"Oh, my, you're back." Silva seated them at a table and gave them menus.

"Sure. We decided to have lunch here. Frank brought his own," Selena said.

"He loves his mate's cooking, but also, she would be offended if he didn't eat it. Do you know what you want?" Silva asked.

Selena read the menu. "I'll have the chicken salad and lemon tea."

"I'll have the beef pot pie and cinnamon tea," Daniel said.

"I'll get them right out." Silva hurried off.

Daniel turned to Selena. "Do you want to go to the same cemetery tonight or a different one? Or do you want to take the night off?"

"I'm getting deliveries in and want to keep working on the shop to start getting it ready. So no cemetery tonight. I should do a grand opening."

"Yes. Everyone does, and they're wildly successful."

"Okay. I'll order treats from Silva's shop." Selena loved giving back to the community.

"I can make some chocolate chip cookies."

She laughed. "A man after my own heart, only I'll be eating them up before customers can have any."

He smiled.

"Double the chocolate chips?"

"Naturally, a chip in every bite," he said.

"You have a deal. I'll make a couple of pitchers of wassail."

After they finished their meal, they said goodbye to Silva and returned to the shop. Daniel and Frank began building the dressing rooms while she took in deliveries and opened boxes out of their way. She decided that, until all the merchandise arrived, she would decorate the top shelves with her own special Halloween and fall decorations and post a sign reading: "For Display Only."

Her howling wolves had come in, and she set two of them in the window—the black one for Halloween, and the copper one for fall, representing the red wolf. Then she put a bunch of orange and burgundy flowers around them, as if they were in a meadow full of fall flowers. She opened another box, and she was excited to see that her six-foot skeletons had come in. She hoped Daniel wouldn't mind helping her put them outside.

Best of all, her hand-carved Howling Wolf store sign had come in, and maybe Frank and Daniel could hang that in the window too. Things were beginning to shape up.

They'd already put up the framed mirror, and it made her shop look so much bigger. She found a box of small skeletons and hung one on each end of the mirror. Then, to her surprise, the MacTire sisters arrived.

"We saw you were getting deliveries. Can we help you with anything?" Laurel asked.

"Sure." The sisters had done a beautiful job decorating their hotel. Selena figured they could help her with her decorating.

They began digging out the three-foot-tall, smaller skeletons, and Ellie said, "Oh, we have to have two of these on our counter and one on the banister for the stairs."

"And one of the ones on the counter can be holding this jack-o'-lantern with the battery-operated candle." Meghan pulled it out of one of the boxes.

"The other skeleton can hold onto this bundle of fall flowers." Laurel set it aside on the counter with the rest of the collection they were going to purchase.

Daniel smiled at Selena.

She found a box of turkeys—soft fabric, hand-carved wooden, with springy legs, ceramic turkeys. She also had ceramic turkey salt and pepper shakers. She set them out for anyone who wanted to buy something for Thanksgiving.

Then Maxine Fox popped in. Her clothing shop was on the other side of Selena's store. Maxine started pulling merchandise out of one of the boxes. "I had to see what merchandise you had. The sitting black cat with the witch's hat is mine. Oh, and this one too that is sleeping."

Selena laughed. She would sell everything before she even opened shop. But she was thrilled that others were interested in her merchandise. And it was unique.

She set a carved pumpkin with a wolf howling on its face in the window and placed a battery-operated candle inside it. Then she filled the rest of the window with purple flowers, sunflowers, and pumpkins.

Silva walked inside and laughed. "I thought I had seen all of you come in here. And what's this?" She motioned to the counter, where all the merchandise was sitting. "All the goodies you're going to purchase? I knew I needed to get in here before you bought everything. Aww, the witch kittens are so cute. Oh, I love these skeletons. I wouldn't sell them in my store, but a couple of them drinking from my teacups? Perfect." She set two aside.

Note to self: buy more skeletons.

The guys worked on hanging her sign in the window as the MacTire sisters made sure it hung properly, and now that Selena's store had a name, it seemed more official.

Frank had made the clothes carousels at home, and he and Daniel brought them in and set them up.

They hung up her outdoor skeletons on the awning, just the way she wanted them. She thanked Frank for the beautiful workmanship and for all that he had done, and thanked Daniel for helping with everything. She paid Frank, and he left. She handed Daniel a string of orange lights to hang in her display window, and they hung them up as the finishing touch.

The ladies were hanging up all the clothes on the carousels, looking at each Halloween and fall shirt, then picking out the ones they wanted. Maxine found one with a black cat wearing a witch's hat, sitting among books and potions. Silva found one with a cat sitting in a teacup. Selena had forgotten she had anything with teacups, but Silva didn't sell clothes, just aprons in her shop.

Then Roxie and Kayla Wolff entered the shop. "Oh, my, Selena's shop isn't open yet, and everyone is buying her out. What about these skeletons? We could put children's ski goggles on them?" Kayla asked her sister.

"Three of them?" Roxie asked.

"Sure."

"And a couple of lighted jack-o'-lanterns. We have pumpkins," Roxie said, "but no jack-o'-lanterns that you can light up."

"Aww, look at the fall T-shirts. The Halloween ones are cute too," Kayla said.

They picked out a couple apiece.

Selena had to stop unpacking boxes to make up sales tickets so the ladies could get back to work, but they just kept emptying boxes until they were done.

"We have a recycle bin out back," Silva said, breaking up the boxes.

Everyone began helping her, and Daniel hauled the flattened boxes out back.

"He sure is a help," Laurel said.

Selena remembered Silva telling her that the MacTire sisters were into matchmaking.

"It would have taken twice as long to get my shop in order if he hadn't been here to help." She still hadn't gotten all her merchandise in, but after the ladies pulled out all the things they wanted, they'd sure put a dent in her merchandise, which was great.

The shop was clean and ready for more boxes of merchandise, but for now, she was done. The ladies paid for their merchandise and then left. Daniel asked her if she needed him to help her with anything else.

"No. I've changed my mind. I'm going to run to the cemetery we went to last night and search it further since I got so much done on the shop today."

"Do you want me to go with you?"

"No, I know where it is, and the work can be tedious."

"Okay, I'm off to work to see what they need me to do, and then we'll have dinner tonight at the Timberline Ski lodge?"

"Sure, that would be nice." Then she could see how they used the skeletons to decorate their gift shop and what else they carried.

This time, her mouth hovered at the edge of his, and he pulled her in with gentle certainty, and they kissed each other.

She smiled. "Tonight at six?"

"Pick you up at the hotel."

IF ANYONE HAD TOLD Daniel he would be decorating a shop for Halloween and fall and visiting cemeteries at night, he would have thought they were crazy. But he'd had a ball when he'd done it for Selena. And seeing how thrilled Selena was and how her expression had brightened was worth it.

He realized after he had left to drop by the sheriff's office, he should have bought something from her shop, but he could do it later. She would have more decorations by then.

He was glad the ladies had dropped in to help and to shop. It had made Selena's day.

Sheriff Jorgenson greeted Daniel. "How'd it go?"

"Good. Except for getting some more merchandise in, Selena's all set."

Peter cleared his throat. "I mean between you and the she-wolf."

"Oh, we're having dinner again tonight."

"Keeping the other bachelor males at bay?"

"You had better believe it."

Peter laughed. "As to sheriff business, I need you to drive up to the lodge. A hit-and-run accident occurred, and I need you to check into it."

"In their parking lot?"

"Yeah."

"I'm on it."

~

DURING THE LATE AFTERNOON, Selena slowly began looking for headstones with any engraving she could decipher at the cemetery she had visited with Daniel, when she heard crunching in the fallen leaves and twigs in the woods. She paused and watched for any movement. She usually wasn't afraid of much, but it just felt ominous, like someone was observing her.

Instantly, she thought about the men out on bail who had stalked her back in Fort Wayne, Indiana. She didn't think any of them would follow her there. But it still came to mind, sending chills up her spine. When she looked around, whoever or whatever it was had stopped still.

Maybe it was a deer. If it were a deer and she walked toward it, it would run. If it were a person...

Chill bumps covered her skin. She wanted to check it out, to reassure herself that it was nothing, but she couldn't shake loose of the fear she had that someone was observing her.

She took a deep breath and began searching the headstones again, only to find a skeleton exposed to the elements. She was beyond excited and called Daniel. "I found a skeleton."

"Right, because it's Halloween. Wait, at the cemetery?"

"Yes, it's just lying on the ground where running water unearthed it. It's an old skeleton—1700s. Can I get permission to examine it?"

"At the morgue? Sure. It's in the hospital basement."

"Okay, I'm going to bag it and take it over there."

"I'll give them a heads up."

She glanced in the direction where she had heard something or someone, but whatever or whoever it was hadn't moved once she had become aware that something was there. She hurried with the bag of bones to her car and drove off, watching her rearview mirror to see if someone was watching or following her, but she didn't see anyone. Maybe she had been mistaken.

When she arrived at the morgue in the hospital's basement, Dr. Featherston introduced himself.

"So what do we have here?"

"Someone who had died and had been buried at an unmarked grave at Southside Cemetery near the silver mines." She carefully washed off the bones and laid them out on the table. "Rainwater had left them exposed so I wanted to examine them."

"Selena Rivers, the forensic anthropologist in our midst. The whole pack is talking about it. I can always use your expertise in cases like this," the doctor said.

"I'm happy to help. He had suffered from a broken ankle and wrist, both of which had healed. But death came from a bullet wound to the head that exited out the back of the skull."

"He might have been accused of cheating at cards or stealing someone's gold or silver claim. Or just fought with someone who was trigger-happy," the doctor said.

Suddenly, a man joined them, camera in hand. "This is Brett Silver, who works for our newspaper, cousin to Darien. His mate is Ellie MacTire. She can sometimes commune with the dead."

Selena's jaw dropped. Wow, what a way to put Selena out of business. Forget studies in forensic anthropology when a ghost could reveal the truth to a ghost whisperer. She was so surprised that Ellie could also commune with spirits.

Ellie bounced down the stairs and gave Brett a big kiss.

"You don't mind if we document this in the newspaper for the town, do you?" Brett asked.

"Not at all." Though Selena wanted to reveal it in her book, she couldn't say no to him when he was the pack leader's cousin, and as lovely as Ellie had been to her.

She took pictures for her book while Brett snapped shots for his newspaper. Then Selena revealed to Ellie what she had determined about the skeleton.

"That's Wolf McKennick," Ellie said. "He remembered his brother shooting him. After that, he was dead. He broke his wrist in a mining accident, but it healed. And he broke his ankle when he was drunk and tripped over some rocks."

"So he was a miner."

"Yeah. Practically everyone in that cemetery was."

"Why did his brother shoot him?"

"Barney McKennick shot him over one of the tavern women. Lucy Jones. He suspects his brother would have gotten the woman after he shot him, unless he had been hanged for murder."

"Fascinating."

"He asked if you could rebury his bones somewhere that's not in a gully during rainstorms. He doesn't want to suffer the indignity of being exposed to the elements when his brother probably isn't."

"Of course."

"We'll hold a memorial for him. You don't need to rebury him. The townspeople will," Brett said.

"I'll be there. Is there anything else you can tell me about him?"

"He had a simple life. Work in the mines, leave to eat, visit Lucy at the tavern, play poker, sleep, start all over again. He doesn't blame his brother for shooting him. If he had been quicker on the draw, but he had a bum wrist, he would have shot his brother and been the one swinging from a tree instead. He wondered what happened to Lucy but figured she took up with some other fellow once he was dead," Ellie said.

That was sad, Selena thought.

"If you find any more skeletons, let me know and I'll try to help you out. Sometimes the spirits have moved on, but sometimes, like in Wolf's case, they are still hanging on."

Brett and Ellie left, and Selena said, "Wow."

"I know. The first case I had like that was when Ellie came and told me the whole history of the dead body, I figured I was out of a job," the doctor said.

Selena laughed. "That was my first thought."

Daniel hadn't had any luck finding the car that had hit the other in the parking lot at the Wolff ski lodge, though he had secured a lot of eyewitness accounts. 2022 Black Mazda, dark-tinted windows, muddied license plate so they couldn't read what it was. Several of the patrons had captured video of the accident and the driver tearing off, nearly hitting a couple of hikers in the parking lot.

He put a Bolo out on it to see if they could locate it in their area. The damage to the other vehicle hadn't been substantial so he wasn't sure why the driver would hit it and run. Still, he suspected he had a suspended driver's license, maybe no car insurance, drunk driving, or using drugs, just multiple issues with the driver of the car that he could think of.

He called Peter to give him an update.

"You know, Selena found a skeleton," Peter said.

"Uh, yeah, at the Southside Cemetery near the silver mines."

"Right. Ellie was able to speak with his spirit and learned more about him."

"Oh." He hoped Selena wasn't upset, feeling that her own work might have been less critical if Ellie could tell her everything she didn't know about the man.

"Brett is running the story."

There went Selena's exclusive story for her book. He hadn't even thought of warning her that Ellie, if she could see a spirit, might take over her investigation.

"Do you need me to check into anything else?" Daniel asked.

"There's another hit and run, sounds like the same vehicle. We need this guy off the road now. He's either drunk, on drugs, or the worst driver ever." Peter gave him the directions, and Daniel hurried off to try to catch up to the guy.

On the way to the second crash site, he called Selena. "Hey, sorry about your skeleton case. I heard Ellie and Brett were there."

She laughed. "Here, I did all that training for nothing. I'm fine with it. Ellie's ability to speak with a spirit was fascinating and gave me more information than I could have ever uncovered, given the few records of that time."

"I agree."

"What about getting exclusive rights to the story?" Daniel asked.

"Oh, I think this will be even more noteworthy. My books are read all over, not so with the newspaper, I'm sure. I have to find lots of skeletons, or other headstones that I can read to add to the book. What are you up to? Have you found the hit-and-run driver yet?"

"No, and from the sounds of it, he hit another car."

"Oh, no. Lousy driver and a menace to everyone."

"For sure. He was headed toward the second cemetery you wanted to check out, but I would stay away from that area for the time being. I'm going in that direction to look for any sign of the car."

"Where is the cemetery?"

"I'm serious. Don't go out there. I don't want to hear that you got in an accident with this guy."

"Okay. I'm not about to."

Daniel gave her the location of the second cemetery. "Remember, I'll pick you up at six."

"Yeah, sure, it sounds good."

Then they ended the call, and she thought of going to that cemetery later tonight after dinner. But for now, she had more deliveries arriving at the store, and she hurried over there to put the merchandise up on the shelves.

To her surprise, she got a call from Brett. "By the way, I'm just giving the details in the newspaper on the skeleton, where it was found, age, not all that Ellie said."

"Why not?" She was surprised.

"We post facts. Since some don't believe in Ellie's ability to speak with ghosts, we leave that out. I believe her, of course. But in your book, you're free to reveal whatever you want."

"Thanks!"

"I called to see if you could show me where you found the skeleton so I can take pictures of the spot."

"Oh, sure."

"Where can I pick you up?" Brett asked.

"At the shop."

"Is this a convenient time?"

"It is." It wasn't close to the second cemetery, so they should be fine as far as not running into the black Mazda.

"I'll be there in a few minutes."

They ended the call. She put out some more clothes on the racks, and then Brett pulled up outside the shop. She grabbed her jacket, locked the door, and joined him in his SUV.

They drove to the Southside Cemetery and, upon arrival, left the SUV. She had every intention of checking out the area where she had heard the sound coming from the woods the last time to see if she could smell if someone had been there—human or wolf.

But first, she needed to show Brett the place where she had found the skeleton.

"The skeleton was sitting right here where rain had washed away the soil covering him. As you can see, rainwater runs over here between the gravestones. Eventually, it could erode more skeletons from the ground."

"We can have some men divert the water." Brett was snapping photos.

"That sounds good. I need to check out a place over here for a moment."

"Another find?" Brett asked.

She hated mentioning it. "I thought someone was watching me the last time I was here. But I could have been mistaken." She still felt spooked about it, like he would still be there.

They checked out the area, and her heart pounded as she smelled that a human had been there recently. "Unless I'm mistaken, that was the noise I heard. A human walking on the sticks and fallen leaves here."

"Watching you."

"Yeah." Just like what had happened to her before. "Have you gotten everything you need?"

"I have. Do you want me to return you to your shop or the hotel?"

"The shop, thanks."

Once Brett dropped her off, she got a call from Daniel. "Did you get the hit-and-run guy?"

"No, but I heard someone was stalking you."

Brett must have texted Daniel about it. "Or he just happened to be hiking and came across me and was curious as to what I was doing in the graveyard. Still, he didn't say anything to me, and it creeped me out."

"I don't blame you—being in a cemetery, being watched by

someone unknown. When you go to the graveyard the next time, whichever one it is, let me go with you."

"You'll be my firepower."

"You better believe it."

She couldn't believe how fast the news traveled in the pack.

"Are you free?" Daniel asked.

"Yeah, sure."

"I want you to take me to the location where you smelled the man."

"All right, sure." She was surprised, but glad that he wanted to learn more about the man, so if he encountered him, he would know who he was.

When they arrived at the location, Daniel smelled around.

"That's his scent," she said.

"It's one of the men who came to the Silver Town Tavern when we ate dinner there."

"The drunk, rowdy guys?" she asked.

"Yeah, the fairer-haired of the three."

She shivered. "Okay, that's creepy. He was the one who had thrown the business card down. He was supposed to leave town. What would he be doing at a cemetery?" She hadn't been near him at the tavern, so she hadn't smelled his scent.

"Did you have a light on?"

"Yeah, because despite our wolf's night vision, seeing worn headstones is difficult without a light." She looked around the area and saw where he had been standing.

"So even though he couldn't normally see you in the dark, when you had a light on, he could."

"Right. I wonder where his other friends were." She began stripping off her clothes.

"I can't imagine they would have been far away unless they dropped him off in the woods to pee or something. What are you planning to do?" Daniel asked.

"See if the others were with him, but farther from this spot."

"As a wolf."

"For sure." She turned into her black wolf. He quickly stripped off his clothes and shifted into a beautiful, dark-gray wolf with a white mask. He affectionately nuzzled her muzzle.

She nuzzled him back, and she loved that wolfish interaction between them. Then, they sprinted through the woods, trying to find the scents of the other men. They soon found the men's scents nearer to the highway. The other man had joined them. He had just wandered farther than the others and had come upon an unusual sight—a woman exploring the cemetery at night.

Then Selena and Daniel returned to their clothes, shifted, and dressed.

"I feel better about it. They were relieving themselves, and one saw me. I'm sure they're gone from here," she said.

"I feel the same way. Are you ready for dinner?"

"I sure am."

Then they headed for his SUV and drove to the ski lodge.

Inside the lodge, stone pillars met high timbered ceilings, and hikers and other guests were sipping drinks in the lobby, while a family of four splashed water at each other in a large, enclosed indoor/outdoor pool. It looked refreshing. A two-sided fireplace had a fire going on this fall night while a big old St. Bernard curled up on a dog bed next to it, getting special treatment from a few kids petting him or her.

Selena glanced at the gift shop where skeletons sat in the display window wearing children's ski goggles. Selena smiled, glad the ladies had bought them and displayed them so cleverly.

They headed for the restaurant, and Roxie greeted them as soon as they entered. "I'll seat them," she told the waitress.

Such exceptional treatment by a co-owner of the lodge and restaurant.

"Where would you like to sit? Overlooking the pool or the mountains?" Roxie asked.

"The pool." Though the view of the mountains appealed to Selena too.

"We have a special membership for the pool so that wolves in Silver Town can swim here, even if they're not staying at the lodge. Members usually use it when hikers are out hiking or skiers are skiing, and the pool is empty."

"That sounds great." Selena thought that once she had a helper at the store, she could go swimming when the pool wasn't busy.

"Maybe we can go swimming here together," Daniel said as Roxie handed them their menus.

"I would like that."

"I guess you haven't caught the hit-and-run driver, or we would have heard back," Roxie said.

"No, nothing yet," Daniel said.

Then Roxie left so they could decide what to order.

"I'm going to get the rib-eye steak dinner," Selena said.

"Salmon for me." Daniel closed the menu and watched the family of four—parents, most likely, and two teenage boys playing with a ball in the pool. "So when are you going to have your grand opening?"

"Saturday. I'm going to get everything ready, and it should be done by then."

"All right. I'll schedule some baking time in."

"I was going to tell you not to put yourself out until you said you were making chocolate chip cookies."

He laughed. "They're the only cookies I know how to make."

"They're the only ones you need to know how to bake, as far as I'm concerned."

They ordered their meals, and not long after, the waitress delivered them to their table.

Everything smelled so good. Selena dug right in.

"So what's been your most harrowing case while you've been a deputy sheriff?" she asked.

"We had a shoot-out with three bank robbers in town. Peter and I were hit, but along with the other deputies and some wolves Peter had deputized, we managed to take them down. We have several citizens who are deputized to help in situations like that."

"Oh, wow, I imagine that was harrowing. I'm glad you both were okay."

"Yeah, it took a while to heal from our bullet wounds. I had nightmares about it for months. What about you?"

"Seeing remains that were a distant cousin's was pretty shocking to me. Her ex-husband had shot and killed her because he didn't want her to have half of the proceeds of the house, bank accounts, and other properties, I later discovered. I believe he didn't want to let her go, either. I never knew them, but her DNA proved she was my cousin."

"That had to be eerie. What happened to the ex?"

"It was eerie. He ended up in prison for life with no possibility of parole."

"If she's a cousin, is she a wolf?"

"Yeah. He was human. I did a background search on her and found she'd been married to a wolf. When he died, her family said she'd vowed never to mate another wolf. She'd been loyal to his memory." She exhaled and said, "I finished up that case two weeks ago. I was ready for a break and a different place to live. At least I've never been shot at over my job, though I've been threatened about my findings and stalked a few times."

"Not if I'd been there."

"It would have been nice to have known you then. I didn't think I would have anything to worry about in a wolf-run town."

Daniel shook his head. "We still have criminal elements, both wolf and human, come through town."

"Just like everywhere."

"Exactly. Are the stalkers a reason for you moving?"

"Yeah."

"If you had issues like that here, you would have the support of the entire pack to deal with them."

"That's good to hear," she said, so glad she had moved here.

They finished dinner, and she checked out the lodge's gift shop to make sure she didn't duplicate what they were selling. Mostly, they carried ski clothes and ski ornaments.

Then Daniel took Selena to her shop where she'd left her car.

"Thanks so much for dinner." She kissed him.

He kissed her back. "My pleasure. If you need me to help you further at all, just let me know."

"I will. Thanks." Then she went inside her shop to put away some more merchandise. Afterwards, she called Brett. "Hey, this is Selena, and I want to put an ad in the paper for the grand opening of my shop."

"We were just waiting for the information on time and date, and it will be front page news, courtesy of the Silvers."

"Oh, wow, thanks. That would be great. Saturday between 2 PM and 4 PM."

"You got it. I'll run by and take a picture of your shop tomorrow, if you'll have it ready by then."

"I will. Thanks!"

"I'll be over around three to give you time."

"Okay, perfect."

Then she called Daniel. "I'm having the grand opening on Saturday from 2-4. Brett's having an ad run in the paper."

"We'll all spread the word."

"Thanks, well, I'm just wrapping up some more decorating before I call it a night. Brett is coming over at three tomorrow so I need to make sure that everything is ready for picture time."

"If you need me, let me know."

"Okay." But she didn't want to bother him with decorating the shop when he had a job to do.

She finally finished what she wanted to do and broke down the boxes. She would take them out tomorrow. She would have finished her work, but tonight she felt spooked about going out into the dark alley since all the other shops around her were closed for the night.

Then she closed shop, locked the door, and was perfectly pleased the way things were going. She sighed. She really needed a box of clothes out of her storage unit because the weather was getting colder than she had expected. And in one of the boxes, she had a Greek Princess Andromeda dress with lots of gold trim, inspired by the mythological woman, which she would wear at the shop on Halloween.

She hopped in her car and headed over to the storage units. In the middle of the various sizes, hers being one of the larger ones for her household goods, she unlocked her unit's door.

And thought she saw the black Mazda with a couple of dents where it had been in an accident or two, parked outside the gate for the storage units. The hit-and-run vehicle?

Her heart pounding, she locked the storage unit, loaded the box of clothes into her car, and called Daniel, but then the vehicle took off. She left the storage unit area and started following the car so she could keep Daniel apprised of the situation.

"What do you need?" Daniel asked, sounding cheerful to hear her voice.

"Sorry to bother you, but I might have found your hit-and-run car."

"Where?"

"At the storage units. It was just parked there outside the gates. It is a black Mazda and has two damaged fenders. Not badly."

"I'm on my way with the troops."

"He just turned on north on Pine Street."

"Tell me you're not following him."

"I am. So hurry up and…"

"Selena?"

Her skin chilled. "I have to pull off. They're slowing down. I think they realize I've been following them."

"Shit. Selena, find a lighted area where there's traffic and people."

"I'll go to the service station." People would be there, and it would be well-lit.

"I'll be there in a minute."

"You're supposed to follow the Mazda." She wanted him to catch the menace!

"The other guys will. I want to make sure they don't follow you to the service station."

"All right."

When she pulled into the service station, she parked by the store. Daniel came rushing up with his police car's lights flashing.

She just hoped the guys weren't watching all this while the others were trying to chase down their car.

She got out of her car, and Daniel joined her, giving her a warm embrace. "What were you thinking?"

"I saw the car and wanted to follow him until you could locate him and arrest him. Anyone would have done what I did to help the police."

He shook his head. "It's late at night. These guys are unpredictable. I don't want you getting hurt."

"Okay."

"I'll escort you to the hotel."

"Thanks."

When they arrived at the hotel, he carried her box of clothes to her room upstairs, then they kissed goodnight, and she knew they were bound to continue dating, the way she felt about him. It helped that he was interested in everything she was doing—

looking through cemeteries at night, running a shop, and even her past as a forensic anthropologist. And she loved that he was a deputy sheriff, and that he enjoyed cooking and gardening.

She just hoped the driver of the Mazda she'd been following didn't realize she'd been after him and that she had reported him to the police!

5

Thinking of the danger Selena could have put herself in by following that black car, Daniel finally got ready for bed. Unfortunately, they had lost the Mazda anyway, but he was glad she'd been safe. But he couldn't quit thinking about it and worried they could recognize her car when she had followed it, that she had called the police on them, and that they would give her trouble.

Before he went to work in the morning, he would drop by her shop and pick up a drink for her from Silva's shop since he was getting himself one anyway. He just wanted to start his day by seeing her. He called to ask her what she would like, just in case she had already stopped over there and ordered herself a drink.

"Morning," he said over the phone. "I'm delivering special drinks from Silva's tea shop if you haven't had a chance to get one."

"Oh, that would be lovely. A cranberry tea and a scone, if that would be all right."

"You got it. I'll be right over." He dropped by Silva's tea shop and picked up drinks, a scone for Selena, and a pumpkin muffin for himself.

She unlocked the shop door for him. She was wearing sneakers, jeans, and a T-shirt featuring a wolf sitting in the middle of a pile of fallen leaves, one sticking to the top of its head. She looked cute and whimsical, and he liked the look. Before this, she had mostly been dressed up.

She was unpacking more boxes, and he spied the stack of folded ones. "Do you want me to take these to the recycle bin?"

"Yes, thanks. I was going to do it last night, but I was so tired."

"I've got it." He carried the boxes out to the recycle bin and saw Silva coming out with a stack.

"Now if only I had a mate who would do that for me."

Daniel laughed, then returned to the shop. "Do you need me to help you unpack the remaining boxes before Brett comes by to take pictures for the paper?"

"No, thanks. Roxie offered to drop by and help, just in case I'm not done by then."

"Okay, good. Well then, I'm off to work."

She slid beside him, her lips brushing his cheek, her arms wrapping around his shoulders. "Thanks for getting us breakfast."

His fingers traced her spine as he pulled her close. "Promise me you're done with midnight detective work, trailing unknown cars in the dark of night."

"You didn't catch him, did you? See, if I had continued to follow him, you might have."

"No, it's too dangerous. We learned that they've already hit two vehicles. We figured it's a case of road rage. If they had caught you following them, no telling what they would have done."

"All right. I won't follow the car if I see it, just report it to you."

"That's just what I want you to do." Every time he saw Selena, he wanted to see more of her. He certainly didn't want her to get hurt by this business.

He drove off to work, thinking about inviting her over to his place for dinner. She might want a home-cooked meal. She had to eat somewhere because the hotel she was staying at didn't have a restaurant. He couldn't offer lunch as he didn't know what he would be in the middle of at work by then.

As soon as he walked into the sheriff's office, Peter said, "I hope you told Selena not to follow that black Mazda if she sees it again."

"I did. I just can't understand how it could have vanished."

"He knows the roads as well as we do."

"That's what I was figuring. A wolf then?"

"I don't know. The thought had crossed my mind. As to other news, I got a call from the manager of the Silver Town rental storage units about a break-in. I'll need you to check that out."

"Do you know who rents the unit?"

"Selena Rivers. Her household goods are in there, so you'll need to have her inventory them to see what, if anything, was taken. I hate to report that some things were broken."

"Just Selena's storage unit was broken into?"

"It seems odd, as if she were targeted for some reason. Or they could have gotten spooked and left before breaking into any other unit. But hers is in the middle of a row, which makes me think they went after only hers."

"What about security camera footage?" Daniel asked.

"All knocked out before the perps hit her unit."

"Hell."

"Yeah. It's not the welcome we want newcomers to Silver Town to have."

"I'll give Selena a call and get right on it."

"I figured you would want the case. Good luck."

Daniel tried calling Selena, but it went to voicemail. He'd wanted to know if she wanted to meet him at the storage unit or for him to pick her up. She was probably so busy, she didn't hear her phone. He got into his SUV and drove to her shop.

~

SELENA WAS HANGING MORE sweatshirts on the carousels when the shop door opened. She'd left it unlocked for when Roxie arrived, but the three drunken men who had gone to the Silver Town Tavern the night she had dinner with Daniel sauntered in instead.

"My store isn't open yet." The closed sign was lit up. She suspected they had an ulterior motive and had no intention of shopping in her store. Her body chilled with anxiety.

The sandy-haired man picked up a porcelain jack-o'-lantern from a box that had an old-world mottled appearance. She had five of them and really thought they would go well in the shop. Her gun was in a locked drawer behind the counter so she couldn't reach it. Her phone was in her pocket, but she was afraid to pull it out and escalate a confrontation with the men when they refused to leave.

Then her phone rang, and she fished it out of her pocket. *Daniel.* Just who she needed to speak to.

"Don't answer it," one of the darker-haired men said.

"If I don't, he'll assume something is wrong."

"Don't. Answer. It," the man reiterated.

The sandy-haired man walked around the store, still carrying the jack-o'-lantern, and she knew he had no intention of buying it.

"What do you want?"

"You had your boyfriend force us out of the Silver Town Tavern the other night," the man said.

"He's a deputy sheriff. He did that of his own accord." She didn't believe that was the only reason they were here.

"You put our dad away for life."

Now she understood. It had to do with one of her forensic cases. Who would even have thought someone would come all the way from Fort Wayne, Indiana, to harass her in Silver Town?

"Who is your dad?"

"Benny Whittington."

The ex-husband of her distant cousin. She'd been murdered in cold blood because of a contentious divorce. Instead of just dividing the property they had together equally, he wanted all of it and ended up in prison for life, getting none of it.

"I only shared the facts of the case concerning a forensic analysis of the murdered victim's bones. The detectives pieced the rest of the case together." But she had proven the ex-husband had injured her multiple times, with the injuries healing, but traces of the damage still showing. Which was why she had finally left him, and he couldn't handle it.

Selena did not doubt their father's guilt.

"Her boyfriend is likely to check on her when she doesn't answer her phone," the other dark-haired man said.

When she observed them closer, she thought the three of them were brothers. But they were all human. Her distant cousin would have been a wolf and would have had to have been their step-mother. She had never heard of her cousin before. There was never any mention of Benny having sons in the news reporting on the case, and they were never seen in the courtroom.

Maybe that's why the boys had no empathy for her death—she was just the stepmother. She had only married Benny two years earlier, and the men appeared to be in their thirties, so she wouldn't have raised them.

The blond-haired guy smashed the jack-o'-lantern on the wood floor, where it crashed and broke into a million pieces, infuriating her. Then the youngest man grabbed one, too, and smashed it, as if he had to prove he was tough, too.

She wanted to smash both of the men!

"Your dad can appeal his conviction."

"He is, no thanks to you."

Roxie came to the front door, and the men hurried out the back door. Selena rushed after them. They got into the black Mazda with the damaged fenders and tore off. *The hit-and-run vehicle.*

"What in the world happened here?" Roxie asked as Selena returned to the shop and locked the back door.

Selena frowned at the broken jack-o'-lanterns. "Don't touch them. They're part of a crime scene."

"What?"

Daniel drove up, parked, and headed inside the shop. At once, he saw the broken pumpkins. "What has happened here?" He pulled her into his arms and gave her a warm embrace.

She appreciated it after what she'd been through. "Three men came into my shop. The same three men who arrived drunk at the Silver Town Tavern."

"And I chased them off?"

"Roxie did. But they're also the ones driving the black Mazda. They drove it down the back alley to stay out of sight."

"Hell. Your storage unit was broken into. I came to get you to inventory what, if anything, was damaged or stolen. I haven't been there yet. But if they're driving the black Mazda and it was outside the gates of the storage units, were you getting some things in there?" He gave her a tighter squeeze as if protecting her from the threat.

"Yeah. I grabbed the box of clothes that you carried into the hotel later and saw the Mazda." She hugged him back, so glad he was here and that Roxie had scared the men off. Though she wished they had been arrested.

"So they knew which storage unit you had rented."

"Right." She was being stalked again, which totally unnerved her. "They broke my jack-o'-lanterns in the shop and then when Roxie entered the shop, they took off. I'm sure they were afraid you were coming because they wouldn't let me take your call."

"Roxie, I want you to leave," Daniel said.

"But I was going to help Selena get ready for picture taking."

Daniel was calling in the new incident to Peter. Then he said to Roxie, "I need to take Selena to the storage unit to see if anything is missing. I don't want anyone here who is unprotected in case the men return. I'll help her with the rest of her merchandise."

"All right, but if you need more muscle, my brothers can provide it," Roxie said.

"Thanks, Roxie," both Daniel and Selena said.

Selena was glad that Daniel was also concerned about Roxie's welfare.

Then Roxie left, and Selena locked up her store.

"Has this anything to do with you following them?" Daniel asked, sounding worried.

"You know that case that I told you about where my distant cousin was murdered by her ex-husband? Those were the man's sons."

"Ahh, hell. So they believe you're responsible for putting their father away in prison."

"Yes. He's appealing his conviction, but it's a solid case. I doubt he can get off."

"So what do they want you to do about it?"

"They didn't say. I suspect they weren't sure what to do. When you called, they wouldn't let me answer it. I told them you were a deputy sheriff and that you were coming to see me. So I think that spooked them."

"Good. But I hated to learn they were here, harassing you."

"Do you think they're the ones who broke into my storage unit?"

"Yeah. We'll have to match up their scents with the men in your shop, who were the same ones I confronted. Your storage unit was the only one broken into, and they tampered with the security cameras, disabling them, so we don't have any surveillance footage. But smelling their scents at the location will be enough."

"Great."

"On a brighter note, do you want to have dinner with me at my place tonight?"

She smiled. "Yes. I would love it. That's the problem with staying at a hotel without a private kitchen or a restaurant. You have to leave the hotel to eat out all the time. So a home-cooked meal would be great."

"How about beef stroganoff made from scratch?"

"Yes, it sounds delightful." She was glad he could cheer her up after the confrontation with the brothers.

They arrived at Selena's storage unit, where yellow crime scene tape had been strung up. The bastards had broken a set of her mother's dishes and rifled through files, probably looking for documentation to discredit her testimony on the witness stand.

"I'm sorry about the dishes."

"There wasn't any reason to break them." Her eyes misted with tears. "But I definitely smell the three men's scents."

"Yeah, it's them."

She noted another box of files had been taken, related to other cases. They probably had gotten spooked about staying too long at the storage unit and figured they would look through the files somewhere else, where they wouldn't get caught.

"One box of files is missing, but nothing related to their dad's case."

"Why not take the box of files that has their dad's case in it?"

"I imagine they were nervous about being caught and quickly rifled through it, but didn't see it. So they left it behind."

"Okay. That makes sense. I often overlook something I'm trying to find when I'm in a hurry, and it's right there."

"Yeah, me too. Then, thinking it wasn't in the first box, they grabbed the second one, believing it would have the information. But the thing of it is, all that information I had on their dad was shared at the trial."

"They're vengeful amateurs." Daniel took photos of her broken dishes and the box with the files that had been rifled through. "Do you need anything from here since we're here?"

"We'll take the file for their dad's case to safeguard, and I have three boxes of fall and Halloween decorations I can use to decorate my shop further."

"All right. Which ones?"

She pointed them out, then he helped her haul the boxes to his SUV. "I'm concerned that since the men know where your household goods are, and they know about your shop, they could know that you're staying at the Silver Town Hotel."

"Do you have any suggestions?" she asked.

"That you stay at my place?"

That's what she figured he would say. "All right." He was a deputy sheriff after all. And she could cook at his house so she wouldn't have to eat out all the time. She would thoroughly enjoy his company further.

He looked surprised that she would so readily agree. "Really?"

"Of course, I feel pretty safe at the hotel, but after the men confronted me at my shop, broke into my storage unit, and knowing they are the hit-and-run drivers, I would feel safer at your place, with you."

"I'll have someone park your vehicle somewhere safe and out of sight. You can duck down when I take you home. Someone will be at the shop while you're there, and we'll have someone drive by it periodically to make sure it's not vandalized or broken into when you're not. I still can't imagine why they would believe only you had anything to do with putting their dad behind bars. The prosecuting attorney, police detectives, other medical experts, and witnesses would all have had a say in it."

"I know. Unless they tried to intimidate the others involved in putting their father behind bars already. Are you sure you're ready to have an overnight guest for a while?"

"Are you kidding? I'm delighted."

"Okay, good. We'll need to drop by the hotel so I can check out."

"I'll have one of the deputies do it so if the men are watching the hotel, they won't know you're leaving there."

"Oh, good idea." She wasn't really thrilled about having someone pack her things, but she understood the reason. "I'll give the ladies a call then." When she called them, Laurel was horrified.

"Should we be worried?" Laurel asked as Selena put the call on speakerphone.

"Not as long as Selena isn't there, but Peter will make sure you ladies are safe," Daniel said.

It helped that Peter was married to Meghan MacTire, though the sheriff's department staff was bound and determined to keep everyone safe in Silver Town.

"I need to give Peter an update on everything," Daniel said.

"So Selena's the target," Laurel said.

"Right. The three men involved were also driving the hit-and-run car," Selena said.

"Oh, no," Laurel said.

"I'll explain everything later, but someone will come and pack up my things, and I'll be staying at Daniel's place."

"We'll pack for you and give it to whoever comes for it," Laurel said.

"Only the good guys."

Laurel chuckled. "That goes without saying."

"We're going back to the store to unload some more decorations. I have those that are for just appearances. I'm not selling them."

"Your own collection then. You'd better put them out of reach."

"I am, and I'll put a sign up saying not for sale."

Then they ended the call, and Daniel drove her to the shop. While there, he took pictures of her broken jack-o'-lanterns before they unloaded the boxes of Halloween and fall decorations from his SUV. Before she could even start unpacking them, she began getting calls from everyone—all the ladies who had approved her application for the store, and both Darien and Lelandi, who were concerned about her feeling threatened.

Also, Peter, who told her he had deputies scheduled to watch her store and storage unit throughout the night. Brett, who told her he would change the time for seeing her, if she needed a later time, and people she hadn't even met yet.

"Wow, I didn't know belonging to a pack had so many perks," she told Daniel as he cleaned up the broken shards of the jack-o'-lanterns. "Thanks for that." She opened the boxes containing the Halloween decorations.

"Yeah. We all have each other's backs." Then he emptied the decorations from the boxes onto the check-out counter.

"We'll put those up on the highest shelf where I would need a ladder to reach." She began making a sign that read: "Personal Items Not for Sale."

He pulled a ladder over to the shelves, and she began handing him the items.

"Your boss is going to fire you for missing work so much." She worried about him taking off so much time from work.

"Nah. You're the key to the hit-and-runs and the break-in at your storage unit and the threats to you at your shop. Even if I weren't dating you, one of us would have been here safeguarding you."

"Okay. That makes me feel better." She was amazed by the service they provided here. If she had been back in Fort Wayne, no one would have safeguarded her like this.

Once they finished placing all her special personal decorations on the top shelf, out of reach of customers, he put her sign there, stating they were not for sale. Then Brett arrived.

Perfect. Just in time for picture taking.

Brett took some pictures from outside and several from inside her shop. And then he took some photos of her at the check-out counter, smiling. "Perfect. I'll develop these and then place them in the ad. Lelandi's having posters made that will be left off at each business also.

"Oh, wow, that's great."

Brett disappeared around the corner, and Selena wrapped her arms around Daniel without warning. "The shop is really coming together, isn't it?" she said, her voice warm against his shoulder. She was nervous about tomorrow and the grand opening, hoping she wouldn't be overwhelmed or that no one would show up on such short notice.

He enveloped her in his arms and kissed her. "You've got a winner."

She loved how affectionate and upbeat he always was.

She felt a little nervous about going to Daniel's home with him. Should she stay in a guest room if he had one? Or stay with him in his master bedroom if he offered it to her? She wanted to, but she was in unexplored territory here. She never stayed overnight at a boyfriend's house.

"Do you want to go to my place now?" he asked.

She put some sale signs up for some of her products as an incentive for the grand opening tomorrow. "Yeah. We're done here."

Then she got into his SUV and ducked down. He drove for what seemed like forever before he finally pulled into a garage. Did he live way out? Or had he been trying to shake off anyone who might have tried to follow him?

Had anyone followed him?

6

Daniel had been glad he'd cleaned up the place before he'd brought Selena home. He'd done so with the idea that he'd ask her over for dinner. He hadn't expected to have her stay at his home, but after all that had happened, she had to stay with someone who was with law enforcement. Peter and Meghan would have offered, but he was glad to be the one to do it, and that she had agreed.

He closed the door to the garage, relieved that no one had followed him. Then the doorbell rang, and he had an eerie feeling it was trouble. "Why don't you wait here for me?"

She nodded and stayed in the car. He went to the front door and found only Peter there with Selena's bags.

"Thanks, Peter."

"No problem. Just keep her safe."

"I will."

Then Peter left, and Daniel went out to the garage to speak to Selena. "Peter brought your bags. So now the question is, do you want them in the guest room or my bedroom?"

She smiled. "If I didn't know better, I would say you set this whole thing up."

He chuckled. "Not me."

"I'll stay in your bedroom, better security that way."

"That's just what I wanted to hear, or I would be up all night worrying about you staying down the hall."

"Do you live way out?" she asked, carrying one of her bags while he got the other two.

"I live out of the way so I can run as a wolf anytime I want. But I took several detours also to make sure I wasn't being followed."

"I guess I can't look for an apartment anytime soon."

"Not until we catch these bastards."

"Okay." She didn't want to impose on Daniel for too long.

When they reached the bedroom, she said, "Oh, how spacious your room is, even with a king-size bed taking up some of the room. I love the big windows on either side of the bed, which offer views of the forest. The windows make me feel like I'm outdoors. How pretty." She ran her hand over the bedspread. "I love your bedside tables because they have three drawers each, providing more storage. I had just bedside tables, and I always thought I should have bought ones with drawers to organize things better. Love your highboy and the dresser with a mirror, which makes the room look even bigger. Having everything in ivory makes the room look uncluttered and spacious."

"Thanks. Yeah, I couldn't figure out a color scheme and saw that online, so just went with that. Just touch the lamps on the bedside table and they come on automatically."

"That's cool." She opened her suitcase and wondered if he had a spare drawer or two.

As if he read her mind, he moved some things out of a few dresser drawers. "You're not an imposition. I'll enjoy the company. You can use these drawers, and I'll move the clothes in the closet so you have room. If you need more space, just let me know."

"Thanks. I appreciate it."

He hated living out of a suitcase himself and wanted to make Selena as comfortable as possible. "I'll start dinner."

"Do you need me to help with anything?"

"No, just get settled in, and then you can join me."

She soon joined him in the kitchen, sidling up to his side at the counter, and before he could even finish rinsing the mushrooms, Selena had already commandeered the chef's knife. She cut up the mushrooms, then placed them in the colander.

He watched as she immediately moved on to the onions, rolling one beneath her palm to loosen the outer skin before pinning it with her thumb and drawing the blade through in a single, confident motion. He cut the steak into cubes and placed them in the saucepan. Selena, meanwhile, hummed tunelessly—not a song he recognized, just a low vibration, a sign she was deep in her own process.

He stole glances at her—her hair hanging in massive curls, wild, her face open and intent on the task, her lips parted only when she exhaled, blinking back onion tears. He liked having her help him with a meal. Even in the kitchen's fluorescent lights, with the tile counters cluttered with pans and bowls, it felt homey. He felt like he had a real person in his life, not just a rotation of guests visiting for a good time.

She reached for the container of sour cream and knocked over the salt shaker instead. When he picked it up for her, she smiled and wiped her wet palms on a paper towel. She watched the onions cooking in the pan.

He was used to cooking alone, used to the silent cadence of chopping, heating, seasoning, and plating. But with her there, it was fun.

They worked in concert, trading off tasks without needing to say what came next. She salted the mushrooms with a flourish, then gestured for him to pour in the wine, which hissed and sent up a vapor of earth and alcohol.

He tossed in the meat; she stirred it with a wooden spoon, scraping the bottom of the saucepan. The whole room filled with an aroma that was both savory and made their stomachs growl, a richness that made him want to eat right out of the pan.

Selena leaned against the counter, arms crossed over her chest, watching him finish up. "My foster mom used to make Hamburger Helper out of a box and call it stroganoff. I thought that was the real thing until I was, like, sixteen."

"I won't tell if you don't," he said, plating the noodles.

She smiled, and for a moment, there was no banter, no nervous energy. Just the two of them, standing close in the steam and the bright kitchen light.

Then he spooned out the sauce, and she carried the plates to the table.

"This smells delightful," she said.

"It does. Are you ready to eat?"

"I sure am." She got them ice water.

He added glasses of red wine. Then they sat down to enjoy dinner.

She took a bite. "This is really delicious. So much better than my foster mother used to make it."

"Now you know how to do it."

"I sure do."

After they finished dinner, they cleaned up the kitchen, and then they decided to watch a movie on TV.

"*Wolfman*?" she asked, searching for a movie to watch.

"Yeah, sure. I haven't seen it yet."

They cuddled on the couch together as if they'd been dating for a while. It felt so right.

She ran her hand over his. "Afterwards, we could run in your woods?"

"Absolutely."

They watched the movie, enjoying it, and when it was over, they stripped off their clothes and ran as wolves. She was beautiful to look at with or without clothes, he thought, right before she shifted. And her black wolf coat was striking. He shifted into his gray coat and led her through the wolf door that took them out back and into the woods.

THEY RAN THROUGH THE FOREST, and Selena thought how lovely it was that Daniel's home was backed up against it. She was still smelling the air, looking for any sign of the three men who had come to her shop, though she probably didn't need to. She realized that she was spooked more than she thought she had been. She hated them for making her feel that way.

Daniel nipped at her tail in playful fun, taking her mind off the men. She rounded on him and nipped his neck. He howled with joy. She offered her own howl, showing how happy she was. Now, anyone who heard her howl would know she was with Daniel and most likely realize she was Selena.

He chased after her, and she kept out of his reach for a while. But he soon caught up with her, and she rounded on him again, biting at him as he bit back at her. She kept out of his reach when she bit at him, but he did the same with her.

She darted away from him, and he tackled her in a pile of leaves. Both were wearing leaves stuck to their fur, and she wanted to laugh.

Then they lay down on the grass and leaves and looked up at the sky, at the stars, and at the moonlight, highlighting the way. It was a beautiful night to be out for a wolf run, but she was growing tired.

She licked his face and then rose to her feet. He joined her, and then they raced back to the house. Arriving before she did, he let her go through the wolf door first.

They shifted and began getting dressed. "That was fun." She'd really enjoyed running with Daniel in the cool night air. With other wolves she'd run with, they didn't play with her. This was so much more enjoyable.

"I feel the same. Playing with you was super special."

Then he led her to his bedroom.

"Do you have to work tomorrow? I need to go into the shop and make sure everything is ready for the grand opening."

"I'll go with you until I'm relieved. Then I'll come and help out at your grand opening."

"Okay. I look forward to it."

"Do you prefer one side of the bed to the other?" Daniel asked.

"I'm fine with either side, but I'll take the side you don't usually sleep on."

"Okay. You can shower in here. I'll take one in the guest room."

Once she was finished showering, she dressed in pajamas and climbed into bed, realizing she didn't know which side of the bed he slept on. He could make her move when he got here.

He finally joined her in bed.

"Am I on the right side or wrong?"

He smiled. "You're on the right side."

Then they forgot about sides and curled up together, feeling it was so right. The bed was as big; they could have slept apart, but this was perfect. Never had she met a wolf that she was so into before.

DANIEL HADN'T ENVISIONED ENDING the night like this, but he was glad for it. Selena's body, pressed against his side, radiated a gentle, persistent warmth that seeped beneath his skin and settled deep in his chest. She curled into him with ease, like a cat finding its favorite spot on the sun-warmed windowsill.

He was startled by how completely natural it felt to have her tucked beneath his arm. Her hair spilled over his shoulder and tickled his neck, making him hope they could spend a lot more time together like this—sharing meals, playing as wolves, snuggling in bed together at night.

At first, he'd feared awkwardness—the inevitable shuffle of limbs, the pressure of two people pretending not to notice the intimacy of their arrangement. Instead, there was a slow, organic choreography: Selena turned, he adjusted, and soon it was as if his bed had always been meant to contain the two of them, a matched set.

He tried to play it cool, to keep his breathing unhurried, but he was keenly aware of the minute movements of her fingers as they traced lazy patterns on his bare chest. Their pheromones were already dancing around each other, showing their keen interest in one another. For a few seconds, he wondered if she was even awake, or if she was sleepily lost to the world, the way her breath had softened and steadied. But then she looked up at him, her eyes glimmering with something between amusement and relief.

Daniel realized that he didn't know what came next, and for once, he didn't mind the uncertainty. He felt the tension that had colored his evening soften at the edges, replaced by a fragile sense of promise. There was something in the air—a hush, a pause, the possibility of something real which he wanted to continue to explore. He let himself enjoy it, the quiet miracle of her closeness.

She was so cuddly and fit him perfectly.

He finally fell asleep and woke to the aroma of coffee brewing in the kitchen. He was surprised she had left the bed and hadn't woken him. He dressed in his uniform and then joined her in the kitchen.

"I hope you don't mind that I made the coffee," she said, dressed in a skirt, sweater, and boots for her grand opening.

"I must have been tired. I didn't even feel you leave the bed."

"You were. I didn't want to wake you, but I guess you smelled the coffee."

"I did. A surefire way to wake me. Do you want me to fix us breakfast? Sausage or ham? Hash browns? Toast?"

"Ham, hash browns, and toast sound delightful."

"Coming right up."

"Do you have honey?"

"Yes, and strawberry and grape jam."

She poured them cups of coffee, then helped him warm up the ham and popped the sliced bread into the toaster while he made the hash browns. "Scrambled eggs?

"Sure."

Then he figured she'd be all set for her final preparations for her grand opening. He just hoped Peter would let him stay at her shop for the day.

Once he was done cooking the eggs and hash browns, he served them up, and she added ham and toast.

He took the plates to the dining room table while she carried their coffee cups.

Then he called his boss. "Do you need me to take care of anything?"

"Are you going to be at the grand opening for Selena's shop?"

"Yes, sir, unless you need me."

"No. I need someone to watch out for Selena, and if you want the job, it's yours."

"Yeah, you know I do."

"Okay, good. One other thing, some of our men found files belonging to Selena. They were scattered all over the woods. They gathered them up. I'll be at the grand opening and drop them off."

"She said they didn't have any files that were relevant to their dad's case."

"Good, then they didn't get any important files."

Then they ended the call, and Daniel began to eat breakfast

with her. "I'll be taking you to the shop and staying with you the rest of the day. Some of our deputies found the files that those men stole scattered in the forest."

She frowned. "I'm glad they found the files, but what creeps they are. I'm glad that you will be at my shop."

"I agree." He didn't even want to think of the mess her files would be in. But he suspected it would be a tangle to straighten out.

They finished breakfast and then cleaned up the dishes. "Are you ready?" She sounded anxious, and he didn't blame her. She was eager to get this over with and hoped it would have a good turnout. With a wolf-run town, he knew it would.

Sure enough, as soon as they arrived at the shop, the MacTire sisters came to help out in case she needed any assistance.

More boxes were delivered that morning, so she was glad to have their help. And they all began putting the merchandise up on the shelves and racks, while Selena stuck price tags on it.

"We're going home to make some treats," Laurel said.

"I need to make those chocolate chip cookies," Daniel said.

Ellie smiled at him. "A man after my own heart."

Daniel laughed. "But you'll have to come home with me, Selena, and we'll have lunch, then return to the shop."

"Sounds good," Selena said.

At lunchtime, they locked up the shop and the MacTire sisters returned to their hotel, while Daniel and Selena went back to his home.

"How about grilled ham and cheese sandwiches?" Selena said.

"Sure, that would be good." He got the ingredients out for the chocolate chip cookies to make seventy-two.

She began making the sandwiches and grabbed a couple of individual packages of potato chips. Then she plated them.

They ate the sandwiches and chips, then he went back to making the chocolate chip cookies while she cleaned up the pan that she had used to cook the grilled ham and cheese sandwiches.

She helped him with the cookies, and then he put them in the oven to bake. But he had to bake several dozen before he was done.

She was already eating one of the ones hot out of the oven, the chocolate chips all melty.

He smiled and bit into one also. "I made enough for you to keep some for yourself."

"What if we run out at the shop?"

"Other food will be there."

"Or we can make more when we get home."

"Sure, we can do that." He ate some more.

She did too. "Okay, I'm ready to go back to the store."

She sounded worried that they wouldn't get back on time, but they still had another hour to go.

"All right. Let's go."

What they couldn't believe was that there were cars parked outside of her shop already.

"I feel like I'm late."

"You're early. So are they. Customers just want to make sure they can get a look at your merchandise before anyone else can."

Then Brett came with a big sign for the grand opening and helped Daniel hang it.

As soon as the Silvers arrived, they had the ribbon-cutting ceremony. And then Selena invited them into the shop.

A table was set up in front of the shop so guests could have food and drinks while shopping.

"I love the way you decorated it," one woman said.

"It's beautiful and just what we needed," another said, carrying some Halloween decorations in her arms.

"Yes, I'll be here a lot," another said. "You have some adorable things. Love your personal display also."

Selena glanced at Daniel and saw him eating another chocolate chip cookie. He looked sheepish. She smiled, wanting another cookie too, but she didn't want to eat in front of all the customers.

The guests began picking out merchandise, and she thought this was going to be a fantastic sale day. She just hoped that it wasn't just one day, and tomorrow, and the rest of the days, she would continue to sell.

But the more time she spent selling items, the more she thought she was in the right place to have opened a shop.

She was so busy checking people out that Daniel began packing up their belongings and carrying them out to their cars.

Silva and the MacTire sisters were helping to serve punch to the customers. Roxie and Kayla were showing customers different merchandise.

Even though she thought they would be done by four, more customers kept coming. Some were humans, not local. That was beneficial because they would be passing through, and she would have more sales as a result. She glanced at the chocolate chip cookie plate, and nothing but a few crumbs were left. She sighed. They would have to make more tonight.

When the last customer left and the ladies who had helped her went home, Selena said, "The shop is a mess."

"Yeah, but you sold a ton of merchandise," Daniel said.

"Yeah, it was great. I'll have to buy more merchandise and straighten up the shop."

"Tomorrow. We'll take care of it then. I think you have a great shop full of merchandise that everyone wants. We'll go home and eat dinner now."

"And make more chocolate chip cookies."

He chuckled, then drove her to his house while she ducked down and pretended not to be in his SUV.

"It was a success," Selena said.

"It was. Would you like some steaks on the grill to celebrate? I have corn on the cob that I can grill too. And champagne I picked up for tonight."

"That sounds like a winning combination. I'll make some more cookies while you're doing that."

"Just don't eat them before dinner's ready."

She laughed. "Like you were eating them at the shop?"

He smiled. "I'm addicted to them, what can I say?"

"I know. Me too. I would have been snacking with you if I hadn't been selling merchandise. Though Silva's meatballs were great. I had to grab one of them before we opened. Do you want to go to another cemetery tonight?"

"Are you a workaholic?"

"I'm just so excited about making all those sales. I won't be able to sleep after dinner right away."

"I totally understand. We'll enjoy a starlit walk through another cemetery."

Then he began grilling the steaks and corn on the cob while she made a salad for dinner and started baking cookies for dessert. She was so glad he was agreeable about another stroll through a cemetery. She didn't figure most men would be.

Once they sat down for dinner, she asked, "When Peter brought in the files they found in the woods, they smelled of the three brothers' scents."

"They did, which confirms they broke into the storage unit and took them."

"Exactly. The food is excellent," she said, taking another bite of the steak. "And the corn is nice and sweet."

"Your avocado, spinach, and mushroom salad hit the spot."

"You have to have your greens." They drank a toast to each other in celebration of her grand opening.

Then, after eating dinner and cookies, they headed over to the second cemetery, and it would make her night perfect if she found something important there.

7

Daniel wanted to do everything Selena wanted, though he would have been happy to just go to bed with her after a wild day at the shop. He was afraid she would find another skeleton if they went to a cemetery and want to identify it before they went to bed.

When he arrived at the location, they got out, turned on their flashlights, and began searching the graveyard. This one was still built in the 1800s, but newer than the other one.

They searched for about half an hour when she found a skeleton. "Ohmigod, it's new, like a month old. It hadn't been buried, which allowed it to decompose faster than if it had been more protected. And the distinctive odor of those three men is here."

"Like father, like sons?" This was so not good. Daniel was glad to find it, but worried about their safety. He got on his phone and called Peter. "We just found a skeleton at the Northside Cemetery —a relatively new one. Not ancient like the others. The three men we're after were here."

"Don't tell me that they murdered someone and dumped the body," Peter said.

"Or they just happened to come here, while the skeleton

had been here for some time and had nothing to do with it." But Daniel wasn't really feeling it. He just wanted to collect the skeleton and get out of there before they ran into anyone unsavory who might still be there and not want the skeleton found.

"Come on, let's go." He tried to keep the panic out of his voice, but he didn't want to risk Selena's safety. He took pictures of the skeleton and its location.

They searched the area, looking for other clues, but didn't find any. There were no clothes there, just the skeleton, and he was certain the person hadn't died there. He would have smelled a hint of decomposition in the area.

They collected the bones, put them in a body bag, and headed for the SUV, but heard a noise in the woods. He dropped the skeleton off in the vehicle and locked the doors. He turned off his light, and she turned hers off. The perps shouldn't be able to see them in the dark, but they might know where his vehicle was parked.

"I'm going to turn into my wolf," she said.

"What about the bones?" He didn't want anyone to break into his SUV and grab them while they were off exploring.

"If the men are still here, I want to go after them so we can identify them. We won't let them return to the bones."

"All right. Me too." However, he didn't want Selena in any danger.

"Are you sure?"

He nodded. "Yeah. We're safer in our wolf coats. They won't be expecting anyone moving around in the dark as a wolf."

"Right."

They made sure they were in darkness, with no moonlight shining through the trees' branches, and then he and she stripped off their clothes and shifted into their wolves.

He stayed with Selena as they smelled the men's scents and set out to find them. He wanted to tear into them, but they had to be careful that they didn't turn them into one of their kind.

Then they would have to kill them anyway.

They smelled the men this way and followed their scent until they reached the road. But their vehicle wasn't parked on the side road either, and the men were nowhere in sight. He nudged Selena to go with him, and they returned to their clothes, shifted, and dressed. Then they hurried to his vehicle.

"Had they found the bones at the cemetery, gotten spooked, and then left them there?" she asked, climbing into the vehicle.

"Or they are the ones who left them there. They might have planned to bury them, figuring no one would ever come to the old cemetery and discover them, but they heard us coming and took off in a hurry." The guys were no good so he wasn't sure if they had anything to do with the bones or not. He started up the SUV.

"You know what this means?"

"We're off to the morgue. Do you want me to call Ellie?"

"Of course. She can be indispensable, though she might not appreciate being called on this after helping at the shop for so long."

"She won't mind. Not as important as it is to know the identity of the skeleton." He called Ellie.

"More bones?"

"New ones this time."

"Oh, not good. Hold on." Then Ellie got back on the phone. "Brett's bringing me."

"Okay, see you there." Daniel called Dr. Featherston after that.

"Another skeleton?"

"Yeah, at the cemetery, but this one is a new one, not centuries old."

"Oh, that's bad news."

"It sure is. We'll meet you at the morgue."

They all arrived at the hospital at about the same time and went down to the morgue in the basement.

Selena laid out the bones and said, "The skeleton's a female. Her neck was broken due to strangulation. She's in her twenties and never had children."

"You can get more than me this time," Ellie said. "Her spirit has gone. Nothing comes to me at all."

Selena supposed that was good. To be stuck in this world after being murdered would be awful. "So we don't know her name or where she was from. She's not a wolf, though DNA would show she was only a human, even if she were a wolf." Just like when she was in her wolf form, she would only show wolf DNA. It kept them safe from experimentation. But as far as scents went, she didn't smell like a wolf.

"I don't know her," Daniel said.

"Neither do I," Brett said.

"Nor do I," Ellie said.

"A stranger. If the three men brought her here, she might not have been here when she died." Selena examined the bones further.

"Why bring her here?" Ellie asked.

"It's probably far enough out of the way from where they killed her, whoever did so. A lot of people who come through Silver Town think it's out in the boonies since we don't have any towns close by, but we have so many wolves who can discover trouble like this. How long has she been out in the elements?" Daniel asked.

Selena rubbed her forehead in thought. "If she had been left out in the elements, warm temperatures, she could have decomposed in a month."

"We have to catch these men and learn the truth," Daniel said.

Brett shook his head. "Yes, before we find anything further that these men could have done."

"We can't do anything more here tonight," Selena said.

"Sorry that I couldn't help further," Ellie said.

"I'm glad she's at peace."

"Me too," Ellie said.

Then they put the bones in storage and left the hospital to return to their homes.

"I hope we can soon discover who she is and where she belongs."

"It's too bad Ellie wasn't able to help more." Daniel wished she could have cleared up the mystery.

"I know. I'm glad she found peace, but it would have really helped to know who she was and who killed her if we could get that information."

"I'm sure we'll figure it out."

When they arrived home, they got ready for bed. Then they climbed onto the soft mattress. They soon snuggled together. This felt so right.

He kissed her on the mouth, and she kissed him right back, her lips lingering against his. He made her feel sexy, and she was ready to do more than just hug and kiss soon.

THEN THEY CUDDLED and finally fell asleep, despite worrying about the possibility of murderers on the loose in Silver Town. When she woke, she glanced at the time and realized she needed to get to the shop and straighten it up before she opened this morning. "I have to get ready to open the shop."

She didn't expect to have much business today, but she still needed to be prepared in case anyone dropped by. Though she really would have liked to have snuggled with Daniel longer.

"I'll take you over there. I'll be staying with you for the day, pick up some breakfast for us, and help you get your shop back in shape."

"Thanks. I don't want to look at the mess it is."

"We'll straighten it out. Before long, it will look as good as new," Daniel said.

"Yeah, but it will be half empty."

"You'll fill it up again."

She loved how positive he always was.

Then they drove over to the shop, and when they arrived, she was right. The place was a disaster. She began cleaning up the trash while he moved merchandise around to fill in the gaps. She took a break to buy some more merchandise while he ordered breakfast for them. He was so cute, helping her out, buying them breakfast. He was the perfect boyfriend.

Silva brought over cups of tea and scones. "I figured you wouldn't want to leave Selena alone so I brought the food and drink over."

"Thanks, Silva," Daniel said.

"Oh, my, your shop is empty, Selena—which is a good thing." Silva glanced around at the half-empty store.

"Yeah, I've been ordering some more merchandise, though I don't want to order too much and then not sell it before I start decorating for Christmas," Selena said.

"All the businesses have posted about the new shop in town so you should be able to get some more customers."

"Oh, that's wonderful." Selena looked through her sales records to find which items had been most popular, then ordered more of those.

"You did a great job on ordering items that no one else had," Silva said. "Well, I'm going back to my shop. Enjoy."

"Thanks, Silva. Breakfast smells great," Selena said.

Then Silva left, and Selena and Daniel began eating the scones and drinking the tea.

"This is good," Daniel said.

"It sure is. It's wonderful being able to have breakfast from next door if I'm running late."

"Yeah, because it's so good."

"For sure."

Once they had eaten breakfast, they got back to straightening her shop up. It looked so barren compared to what it had been when it was stocked to the brim for the grand opening. But that was good anyway, that she'd had so much merchandise to choose from.

"It looks great, as long as nobody buys the other half of your store out."

She laughed. "Then I can start all over again, but with all new merchandise."

"That's the way to keep them coming back." Daniel pulled her into a warm embrace. "Don't worry about keeping your store going. You don't have anything to be concerned about."

But she did worry. What if the big grand opening was it?

Then a group of five people came into the shop. One of the two women said, "We missed your grand opening because we were hiking, but before we leave Silver Town, we wanted to stop by."

"Oh, I'm thrilled. Feel free to browse."

They soon picked out some items—fall sweatshirts and Halloween items—and then purchased them and left.

"Well, that was good." She was relieved to have made more sales.

"See?" Daniel said.

Then more people trickled in and purchased several items.

She continued to have a few sales throughout the day and was thrilled.

"See? You're doing well."

"Not like yesterday, but if I continue to have regular sales like this, I should be able to keep the store open."

They had tuna sandwiches for lunch, and she said, "By the way, what do you think about checking the cemetery out again?"

"No. Peter and the deputies will be searching for the men, looking for more skeletons and any other clues that the brothers had been there."

"Their scents."

"You didn't find any fingerprints on the bones. They had to have been wearing gloves," Daniel said.

"So they were prepared somewhat. They just didn't expect that we could smell their scents."

"Right. What would you like for dinner?" he asked.

"Spaghetti?"

"You've got it."

"So how long before we can get back to a cemetery to look at it?" she asked.

"A few days, I imagine. No one wants you facing those men again while they're on the loose. It doesn't matter that you have a gun," Daniel said.

"You're right."

"You'll be here for a long time so you'll have all the time in the world to write about the cemeteries. In the meantime, you can enjoy the time with me."

"I know I will. I'll concentrate on the shop for now."

"Perfect."

The shop was now officially closed for the night, and she was eager to enjoy the time with Daniel. "Let's go home and eat."

"I'm looking forward to it."

Then they went home and worked on the spaghetti together. She loved making meals with him in his large kitchen with a super large island that worked great for preparing meals and cookies.

"Parmesan cheese?" she asked.

"In the fridge."

She brought it out, surprised at how well stocked his fridge and cabinets were. Like his bedroom, the cabinets were all off-white, and all his appliances were stainless steel. It was a dream working in his kitchen. Even though she'd owned a home in Fort Wayne when she lived there, it had been small and everything had been compact, including her kitchen.

He finished making the noodles. She helped with the hamburger sauce and with cutting up the tomatoes, mushrooms, garlic cloves, and onions.

Then he drained the noodles and plated them. She scooped up the sauce and added it to the noodles, then sprinkled Parmesan cheese on it. They placed the plates of spaghetti and glasses of wine on the dining room table.

"To another successful day at the shop." He toasted her with his glass of wine.

She drank to the toast. "To a lovely day. And a wonderful wolf run?"

"Yeah, I would like that."

"I wonder why the brothers would kill someone. Like father, like sons?" she asked, unable to think of what reason they had.

"Or maybe they didn't kill the woman. Maybe their father did, and they tried to hide her body so that he wouldn't get caught for another murder."

"Oh, I hadn't thought of that. That's a good supposition, but why come here where I am?"

"To get their dad off by getting the file you had on their father, and figured this was far enough from home that they could dump the body at the same time in an old cemetery that no one visits. Until now."

"Yeah, they didn't expect me to explore cemeteries and find the body." Which meant they had to hate her even more if they learned of it.

After finishing their meal, they stored the remaining spaghetti. She came to his side and wrapped her arms around him. "Shall we run in the woods tonight?" she asked, her eyes gleaming with the promise of transformation.

"Nothing I would want more," he murmured against her hair before claiming her mouth with his own.

It seemed he had other things in mind. And he almost changed her mind about going for a wolf run. But she really wanted to run with him as a wolf first, then go from there. Then they stripped off their clothes and shifted. Daniel proceeded her out the wolf door, making sure the way was clear.

He was a true hero.

She quickly followed him outside, and they ran together, playing with each other. She knew she wanted this with him—not just his help and protection, but the meals and wolf runs. The cuddling in bed at night—and more. She hadn't had anything like it with her other boyfriends, and she knew Daniel was so much more special.

Even though she had been considering getting an apartment for the time being, but couldn't with the three brothers on the loose, she was now thinking about how much she would like to stay with Daniel. But of course, he would have to feel the same way.

Then she heard rustling in the fallen leaves nearby, and instinctively, she ran off to check it out. As a wolf, she could run so much faster than a human. But she was hoping it was just a deer.

They were about a mile from Daniel's house, so too far away for the men to know that's where she was staying. Yet it still bothered her that they might learn she was staying with him there.

Daniel ran beside her once he figured out what she was up to. Had he heard the movement also?

She finally reached the spot where the sound had come from—deer, four of them, but they were long gone now. She still felt uneasy about the men learning that she was staying with Daniel. All they had to do was wait for her to go to the shop with him in the morning, then leave the shop with him at the end of the day so they could assume she was living at his home.

He finally nudged at her, indicating he wanted them to return home.

It was time to call it a night. She felt spooked.

They went a long way around, checking their surroundings, then reached the house and bolted inside. If the men had been following them and happened to see them leave it as wolves, at least it would have looked like they had big, scary dogs—maybe wolf dogs—protecting the house and Daniel and her.

Inside the house, they dressed and then headed for their respective bathrooms to shower.

When they joined each other in the bedroom, he said, "It was just deer. I didn't smell any sign of the men."

"Me either. But I did think if they saw us going into the house, or leaving it as wolves, they might be too scared to try and break in and learn if I was staying with you."

He rubbed her shoulder. "I don't want you to leave here, but if you think they'll come after you here and you would feel safer, you could stay with someone else for a while. One of the other deputy sheriffs, or the Silvers even. Any of them would take you in, and all are safe to be with."

"And forgo my nightly wolf run with you?"

He smiled and crawled into bed with her. "You don't have to get an apartment. You can stay with me until you're ready to look for a house. That's after the threat of the three brothers is gone."

It sounded to her like he wasn't ready to declare she was the one for him. Not that she had done so for him either, but she really wanted to be with him exclusively. What if she told him she really cared for him and he rejected her? What if he was only doing this as his job? Then she felt she couldn't stay with him because it could hurt his chances of being with someone else he truly cared about.

Wolves had exclusive relationships, and that would stifle his ability to find his one and only. Though thinking of such a thing hurt her deep down. She even thought staying here wouldn't be worth it. That's how much she was already tied up in how she was feeling about him.

Then they cuddled, and everything seemed all right between them.

"Do you ever think about your long-term plans?" he asked.

Staying here forever if he were in her life. "I love it here," she blurted out. "A wolf-run town, friendly and helpful wolves, you." She sighed. "Especially you." She had never opened up to a guy like that before. But it was true. He was what made her want to stay more than anything.

He smiled.

"What are your long-term plans?"

"Settle down and have a mate, children, and continue to work as a deputy sheriff."

A mate. He sounded like he was still looking for a suitable mate.

"Nice plans," she said, trying not to sound disappointed that he hadn't said what she wanted to hear.

"Yeah. I wanted to propose you stay with me, forgo the apartment for the month, and when you're ready, find a home you want."

That cinched it. She wasn't the one for him. Which meant she wanted to move out right away.

"You know, the brothers probably realize I'm living with you. I think it would be a good idea for me to stay with others until they're caught."

He didn't say anything for a long time. Then he finally said, "All right. I'll arrange with Peter to have places available for you to reside. Knowing him, he and Meghan will have you settle at their home for as long as you want until you feel unsafe and want to move to another home where someone can protect you."

"Okay, good." Then she rolled over to go to sleep.

As if he didn't know how hurt she felt, he drew close and

cuddled with her, but she wasn't in the mood. She didn't snuggle him back and waited for dawn to arrive so she could pack and move to another house.

And start seeing other wolves.

8

Daniel cuddled with Selena, knowing she'd felt spooked on the run, and he didn't want her to feel like that. He also didn't want to give her up to someone else to protect, even though he knew the others would make sure she stayed safe. But if that's what she wanted, he had to let her leave to feel secure until they caught these guys.

In the morning, she was quiet, and he fixed eggs and bacon while she made the coffee. She had gotten up early to pack her bags, and he again felt bad that she didn't feel safe with him. They didn't speak much. She looked tired, like she hadn't slept much last night.

"I'll take you to the shop and then call Peter."

She nodded.

"He'll have someone pick up your bags so if anyone is watching us, they won't realize I'm taking you to the shop and then handing off your bags to someone else."

"All right."

After reaching the shop, he called Peter, who sounded surprised at the new development. "Are you sure nothing is going on between the two of you?"

That had never occurred to Daniel. He glanced at Selena as she opened another box of merchandise that had just come in. He thought she was just tired because she had gotten up so early.

He couldn't remember anything he had said that would have upset her, yet suddenly she wanted to stay with someone else.

"I don't know. I can't remember saying or doing anything that would have upset her."

"Okay, well, I'll relieve you at the store. You can look for the brothers and the Mazda."

Daniel hadn't expected to be relieved at the shop while he watched over her there. "Do you think that's necessary?"

"I do. Meghan's going to speak with her too."

Well, hell. "All right. I'll let Selena know." But he sure didn't want to let her go for anything. Then they ended the call, and he said in a gloomy voice, "Peter is going to watch over you at the store today. Meghan's dropping by, also. Peter wants me to look into these men some more."

"Good." Then she went back to emptying the box.

He cut open the others for her and then heard Peter pull up. He wanted to kiss Selena goodbye, but she didn't appear to be receptive.

"If you need anything, call me."

"Okay."

Then Peter walked into the store. "Keep me informed about what's going on with the investigation."

"I will." Daniel glanced one more time at Selena, who was digging into the boxes and ignoring him. "See you, Selena."

She didn't answer him. Peter raised his brows at Daniel. Yeah, he was in deep shit, and he didn't even know what it was for.

With a heavy heart, he left the shop, worried that if he didn't resolve things between them, she would begin dating other bachelor wolves.

WHEN DANIEL SAID Selena could stay with him and forgo moving to an apartment, but then look for a house, she realized he wasn't seeing a long-term relationship between them, especially when Daniel was okay with handing her off to the other deputies and the sheriff, who would protect her.

She just couldn't even look at Daniel because she'd been so upset this morning over it. Peter helped her empty the boxes of merchandise onto the counter, then broke the boxes down and carried them out back to the recycling bin.

Meghan arrived and smiled cheerfully at her. "Daniel said you got spooked on your wolf run."

"I did. I went to chase off what we heard, but it was only deer. For which I was grateful."

"And no sign of the men's scents?"

"No." She sighed. "Daniel was right there with me." She didn't want Meghan to think he had abandoned her to let her check it out herself. Then she wondered why Peter hadn't returned and worried about him.

Was Meghan here to find out why Selena wanted to stay with someone else? But she didn't want to discuss it with anyone. She would sound like a fool who had gotten her hopes up over Daniel. Yet she couldn't quit thinking of how much he meant to her in such a short time.

"I'm going to the Silver Town Tavern for dinner," Selena said.

"Oh, sure, we can take you."

"No, alone. Only shifters can go into the tavern so I should be safe."

"Why would you want to go to the tavern alone?" Then Meghan's blue eyes grew big as if it dawned on her that Selena wanted to date other men.

Which Selena wasn't really interested in. All she could think of was rebounding after a failed relationship. And how much she missed seeing Daniel. She knew she would compare anything anyone did with Daniel, and they would fall short.

"Okay, well, you still have the issue with the brothers so we'll take you to the tavern and you can sit at a different table."

"All right." She hoped the sheriff's department found these creeps soon. She was tired of always having to be protected and wanted some normalcy in her life.

"I'll bring a soup and salad for lunch for you and Peter, or he'll skip it."

"That sounds great. Thanks, Meghan."

"What are friends for. I'll be back in a couple of hours."

Then Peter came back inside, and she thought it was awfully convenient that Meghan was leaving at the same time. "I'll bring lunch," Meghan told Peter and kissed and hugged him.

He kissed her and hugged her back as if they were newlyweds. "I'll see you in a little while."

AT THE SHERIFF'S OFFICE, Daniel was working on his computer, learning that the three brothers had stolen cars before, which made him wonder whether the Mazda had been stolen. He began searching for any stolen black Mazdas out of Fort Wayne, Indiana, and found one. If it was the same one that had been involved in two road rage incidents without caring how banged up the car would be, he could understand it now.

Jeffry, Logan, and Banyon were the brothers' names, and all had a lot of moving violations, from no car insurance to driving without a valid driver's license to DUIs.

They all worked at a lumber mill, so they were used to heavy-duty work, and they loved hunting. They had pictures all over their social media pages, displaying the deer they had shot.

Then Meghan walked into the office, pulled up a chair, and sat down. "I believe Selena is mad at you. Do you know how that came about?"

"No. We even cuddled in bed last night."

"Was she affectionate back?"

Come to think of it, she hadn't been. He had just wanted to snuggle with her, and she hadn't objected. What had he said or done wrong?

"She wants to go to the tavern," Meghan said.

"I can pick her up at the shop." His spirits brightened.

"She wants to go alone."

"She can't. Not with the brothers still out there causing trouble for her." She needed protection at all times.

"We'll take her, but she wants to eat alone."

He ran his hand through his hair. "I'll meet her there and talk to her and get to the bottom of this."

"I think she might be looking to eat with someone else."

"Hell." He hadn't expected that.

"We could make it so that you get there first and have a table. We'll make sure Silva takes care of it so there are no tables left other than one for us. Selena would have to sit with you or with us."

"Watch her sit with you." Daniel was really disappointed. "I need to figure out what is wrong between us."

"What did you say to her after the wolf run?"

"We talked about long-term goals."

"And?"

"I said I wanted to find a mate, have children, and continue working as a deputy sheriff."

"So you didn't indicate she could be the one?"

"That's what I meant."

"That's not what you said."

He sighed. "You're right. So what do I do now?"

"We'll make sure the tavern is full tonight for dinner, except one table for you and one for us. Then she'll have to sit with you or us. Be sure to have a box of chocolates for her and make it up to her."

"Chocolate chip cookies. She loves them."

"There you go," Meghan said. "See you tonight at six."

Now he just had to say the right things to show how much he cared about her and didn't want to lose her. Six wouldn't come soon enough.

It was half past five when he got a tip that a couple of wolves thought they had seen the black Mazda in the forest, buried by branches. With hope that it was the car he was looking for, he headed out there to verify the find.

WHEN PETER PARKED his vehicle in the tavern parking lot, it was full except for two spots. "It looks like it's full," Selena said, sounding almost relieved, almost disappointed. "Did you make two reservations? I should have thought to do so."

"I didn't think to do so either. We might have to go to the Wolff lodge," Peter said.

But Meghan didn't look worried so Selena thought maybe they were good.

Peter opened the door, and there were two empty tables. He glanced at Meghan. She shrugged her shoulder.

Silva hurried to greet them. "Which table do you want to sit at?"

"I'll take that one since it's for two," Selena said before Peter could respond.

"Uh, yeah, that's fine." Their table was in sight of hers, but not so intrusive that she could speak privately to another wolf.

But when she took her seat, all she could think of was the night she ate dinner here with Daniel and wished she was with him. She glanced around the restaurant, but he wasn't there. Three bachelor males who had said hi to her before glanced in her direction, smiled, but none of them left their seats to join her.

Had they stopped by the table just for show when she had been eating with Daniel? They hadn't been all that interested in meeting her? Or was this more of a case that they felt she was with Daniel, even if she wasn't tonight, and they didn't want to cause friction between them? Well, this was a sad state of affairs.

EXCITED that a couple of wolves on a run had come across the black Mazda, Daniel rushed to the forest to see it for himself, but he wanted to make sure that was the right vehicle before he called for backup.

He parked his car a short distance from where the Mazda was. He could see why the wolves had seen it. The top of the car was sufficiently covered with branches, but the bottom was visible. He smelled the three brothers' scents. One of them had to be the driver of the hit-and-run vehicle.

Daniel reached for his phone to update Peter on the Mazda, when gunfire erupted from the tree line in his direction. His heart raced as a bullet struck his phone, sending it sailing into the fallen leaves on the ground. He was thankful it hadn't hit his hand. In one quick motion, he drew his weapon and dropped behind the Mazda's frame for cover.

Squinting against the muzzle flashes that revealed the brothers' positions among the shadows and foliage, he returned fire into the woods, but he couldn't actually see the men. Damn, these guys were loose cannons.

He howled as a human for help, hoping someone would be near enough to hear him and come to his aid. He couldn't reach his phone safely, though he suspected it was shattered and wouldn't work even if he could.

He sure hadn't expected an ambush, or he would have taken a couple of deputies with him, which made him wonder why the brothers would try to murder him because he'd found the Mazda.

More shots were fired in Daniel's direction, still from the same distance and location. So they hadn't tried to circle him or ambush him. He returned fire, hoping he could incapacitate them. Then a couple of wolves began growling in the direction of the men, and shots were fired at them. He hoped neither of them would be hit. With the wolves distracting the brothers, Daniel finally reached his phone, but it was shattered, and he couldn't turn it on.

Stumbling to reach his vehicle, he finally managed to unlock the car door and fumbled for the medical kit stashed beneath the passenger seat. The blood from his wound had already soaked through his shirt, warm and sticky against his skin. His vision narrowed to a pinpoint of light, then darkness swallowed him whole.

SUDDENLY, Peter got a call at the tavern, and he stood up from the table. He leaned down to kiss Meghan and spoke to her, his face grave. She responded in kind, then he walked over to speak to Selena. "Daniel is in the hospital with a gunshot wound."

Selena gasped. "How bad is it?"

"Bad enough to end up in the hospital."

"Can you take me there?"

"Yeah."

Her heart pounding, she hurried to leave the table, and Meghan went with them. "Where was he shot?" Selena asked, horrified over the news.

"In the right arm. He howled for help, and others went to his aid. He was too far away from this location for us to hear him," Peter said.

"Where was he when he was shot?" She just felt he was invincible and felt terrible that she'd even been considering dating anyone else. Even if he wasn't interested in mating her yet, he'd proved he was a good friend tenfold. And if he never wanted to marry her, she wanted to continue their friendship.

"A couple of wolves found the black Mazda hidden in the woods and called it in. Daniel hadn't taken backup because he wanted to make sure that it was the real deal before he called anyone else in."

"And it was," she said.

"Yeah."

She wiped away tears.

"He'll be all right," Meghan said. "You know how we are with our faster healing."

As long as they didn't bleed out before they could heal fast enough.

They soon arrived at the hospital, and Selena, Peter, and Meghan hurried inside.

"Where is Daniel?" Peter asked the receptionist.

"He's in room four. Doc removed the bullet, and Daniel might be sleeping now. But you're welcome to go in and see him."

They headed for Daniel's room, where they found he was sleeping soundly.

"I'll sit with him," Selena said.

"Let us know when he's awake," Meghan said.

"I will." Selena sat on the chair next to the bed and took hold of Daniel's hand and squeezed. "I'm here for you. And I'm staying with you until you heal up." However, he might not be able to protect her if he couldn't fire his weapon. Then again, she could use hers to protect him. Peter might disagree.

D aniel woke up with a start and found his angel was sitting there, holding his hand. He glanced around and realized he was in the hospital. Then he remembered being shot and howling for help. Aww, hell, he planned to bake chocolate chip cookies and win his she-wolf back over dinner.

"Hey," he said. "You are a sight for sore eyes." He felt they were kindred spirits.

"You found their car but didn't take backup." Selena was scolding him like he had scolded her for following the black Mazda without backup in the first place.

"I don't want you to move out of my house." He wanted to get that out of the way first.

"You wanted me to look for a home of my own."

"You're too precious to me. I had assumed that if you stayed with me instead of getting an apartment for a month, you would have enough time to decide I was yours as you are mine, and forget looking for a house. I wasn't about to let you go."

Tears streaked her cheeks. "I thought you were ready for me to stay with someone else."

He wiped away her tears, choked up a little. "I thought that was what you wanted, and I wasn't going to force the issue. Then Peter threw me a curveball: he said he would watch over you at the shop while I continued searching for information on the brothers. I planned to be there for you during the day at least."

"I didn't want to stay with anyone else."

He smiled. "Then we're thinking along the same line."

She bent toward him, her mouth seeking his. With his uninjured arm, he drew her against his chest in a fierce hold. "I had planned to have dinner with you tonight."

She frowned at him. "Where? At the Silver Town Tavern? Ohmigod, that was a setup." She smiled, amused.

"Friends help friends. They knew I had said the wrong thing to you. Meghan straightened me out and wanted me to smooth things over with you. I was going to make you some chocolate chip cookies, but figured I had to do it after dinner."

She chuckled. "I had such a lovely time with you the first time I was at the tavern with you. I kept wishing you were there. Wait, is that why there were only two tables there for us to use, one for Peter and Meghan, and one for us?"

"That was the plan. I was supposed to be there first, and you would have to choose between sitting with me and sitting with them. I was hoping you would sit with me."

"I had to admit I thought I would be sitting by myself unless a bachelor male came over and asked to join me. But none of them did. They just smiled and didn't come over to the table at all."

Daniel laughed, but that hurt his injured arm.

"What? Don't tell me, they were told not to approach me."

"They knew we are a couple. They wouldn't encroach unless they knew for sure that we weren't a couple any longer."

"And that would have been assured if I had shown up and had dinner with you. But what if I had sat with Peter and Meghan instead?"

"Same thing. They'd still know I wasn't giving up on you."

She smiled. "Yeah." Then she got serious. "But then you got shot. How are you feeling?"

"Dragged out, sore. I can't lie about it."

"So what happened exactly?"

"A couple of our people were running as wolves and came upon the black Mazda buried under branches. The wolves hadn't smelled the scents of the men before, so they didn't know it was tied to them. They immediately howled and then left the scene, afraid the men might be nearby and armed. When they reached their car, they shifted and dressed, then called me because I was on duty at the sheriff's office."

"Then you went out without backup."

"I should have had backup. You're right. I smelled the brothers' scents around the car. I'm sure they'll find their scents inside the car, fingerprints, all of that. One of the men shot my phone out of my hand, luckily missing my hand, but ruining my phone. I howled for help, and a couple of wolves chased the men off."

"So I guess whoever took my clothes to Peter's home will have to return them to your home."

"Our home. We have to wait until I'm out of the hospital."

"Peter might not feel your place is safe enough with you having been shot, but I've got a gun, and I'll protect you."

"The doctor said I have to be here for a couple of days."

She glanced at the couch in the room.

"They'll give you blankets, sheets, and a pillow or two if you want to stay overnight." He was hoping she would stay, but he knew it wouldn't be as comfortable as being in a real bed.

"Yes. I'll stay here."

He was thrilled. "Deputy Trevor will watch the room. They'll switch deputies out for the duration of my stay here in case the brothers think I saw who shot me."

"I can't believe they would shoot you and not kill you."

"I was shooting back until the wolves started chasing after

them. I heard them scurrying through the brush like scared rabbits. I hope I hit one, but I never even saw the men hidden in the trees. They might have thought they were going to scare me away and not hit me. But it doesn't matter what their intentions were. They shot a law enforcement officer, and that is enough to put them in jail."

"Was the car impounded?"

"It was, and they're going over it with a fine-tooth comb for evidence. They found another skeleton—this one under a blanket in the trunk of the car. They want you and Ellie to examine it. They also checked the VIN, and it turns out it was stolen in Fort Wayne, Indiana. I had assumed so since one was stolen there, but the VIN proves it."

The nurse came in to check Daniel's vital signs and made up the bed for Selena. "If you need anything, just let me know."

"Thanks," Selena said.

"And, Daniel, just push the nurse's call button if you need something." Then the nurse left.

"I guess we really are a couple now," Selena said to Daniel.

"Yeah, only a couple would stay overnight together in a hospital room. And hell, I'm glad."

"Yeah, me too."

Then Peter and Meghan knocked at the door. "Just us," Peter said. "I put out the word that you need your rest. However, you know Lelandi and Darien. They'll come by and check on you."

Meghan smiled to see the couch made up into a bed and Selena sitting by Daniel's bed, holding his hand. "We're glad it wasn't worse than it was."

"You and me both," Daniel said.

Then the Silvers arrived. "We've got every available man out looking for these Cretans," Darien said.

"How do you feel?" Lelandi asked.

"Glad to be here," Daniel said. And even gladder to be with Selena and to have resolved the issue between them.

"One of the deputies will be at the shop. Will you be in at all?" Peter asked Selena.

"There's no need for you to sit in the hospital all day tomorrow," Daniel said. "It's important that you continue to sell for your own peace of mind. And you'll be watched, so you'll be safe there."

"I've got to check on the skeleton too."

"I'll call Ellie and have her meet us in the morgue," Peter said. "At least we're already at the hospital."

"Let me know what you find out," Daniel said.

"I sure will when I come back to sleep here," Selena said.

SELENA WANTED to be with Daniel. How would it look if she left him alone in the hospital while she was at her shop tomorrow? On the other hand, she didn't have anyone to open her shop and manage it, and she hated to leave it closed for a couple of days until Daniel could be back home. And then she would feel guilty that he was home alone.

Sitting around the hospital, while she worried about her shop, wasn't ideal either. But she certainly hoped she could help identify the new skeleton.

"I'll go in the morning and open the shop, then come back here for lunch and dinner." By dinnertime, her shop would be closed anyway, and she would spend the night at the hospital again. Plus, she needed to drop by his house, shower, and change, and then go to the shop.

"We have your bags, and you can shower and change at our house," Meghan said.

"I'll be going with you both." Peter saluted Daniel. "Stay out of trouble."

"I'll try."

Then Selena kissed Daniel, and he kissed her back deeply, telling her he wanted to be with her long-term.

She was delighted that things had been clarified between them. Then she left with Peter for the morgue.

Once they were down there, she began identifying the remains. It was a woman, and she was about the age of the first female skeleton Selena had seen in the cemetery.

Then Ellie and Dr. Featherston joined them. Selena and Peter waited to see if she could commune with a ghost. It seemed like forever before she answered. "I don't feel anything from her spirit either. She must have passed on. Sorry, I can't help you this time either."

"I had hoped you could solve the mystery of who they were and who killed them. But how was another matter. She was shot in the head just like the other woman. I'll have to check for fingerprints on her bones, and I'll do a facial reconstruction for both women. We'll need to share photos of the reconstructed faces to see if anyone knows them. If they were from Fort Wayne, Indiana, we might be able to find two women who went missing there, since the brothers are from there."

"I'll get on that right away," Peter said. "Are we done for now? I'll take you to the house, and you can shower and change clothes. I've got your bags in the car."

"Perfect and thanks, Ellie," Selena said.

"I wish I could have been more help."

"I love your special gift," Selena said.

Then they all left, and Peter took Selena to his home while Selena lay down in the back seat of the car. Then they drove into the garage.

"The guest bathroom is on the second floor to the right," Peter said, carrying her bags into the house.

Selena grabbed one while Peter took some more business calls in another room.

"Do you want decaf coffee and a cinnamon roll before you return to the hospital?" Meghan asked.

"I would love that. Sugar and cream with the coffee, please. I'll be right out." Once Selena showered and dressed, she felt great.

When she reached the first floor, Meghan had fixed a cup of coffee and placed a cinnamon roll on a plate for her.

"I'll have another cup of coffee with you."

Peter was still talking in another room.

Meghan explained, "He's getting the latest information on the shooters. They collected the rounds, including those that Daniel had fired. Sixty rounds were fired in all. Luckily, the wolves who came to his aid weren't hurt. They were the ones who had discovered the car, and when they realized Dainel was alone, they stayed near their car to be his backup in case he needed them. They're the ones who called in that he'd been wounded."

"It was a good thing they were there."

"Yeah, when they heard all the gunfire, they knew he was outmatched in firepower."

Selena shivered, thinking Daniel could have been hit several times and not lived through the barrage. But she was glad that the wolves were fine and had bravely taken on the gun-wielding assailants, chasing them off so they could get help for Daniel.

"Now the police just need to find the guns and match the shell casings with them," Meghan said.

Selena took a sip of her coffee. "Here, we thought the father had killed the women. But these men have killer instincts too."

"Their father still might have killed the women, but when Daniel saw the car, they thought they could get rid of him and then move the car. Now they're stranded until they can steal another vehicle. And they've been caught transporting two skeletons across state lines, if the first one has anything to do with the brothers."

"True. Maybe they'll catch them then. How did they steal the Mazda in the first place?" Selena took a bite of her cinnamon roll.

"The owner left the car running at a service station convenience store. She ran inside to grab a soda, and the men took off with her car." Meghan drank some more of her coffee.

"That will teach her to leave her car running and unattended."

"For sure."

Selena finished her coffee and cinnamon roll. "Thanks, that was really good."

"You're welcome."

Peter ended his call and left the room. "Are you ready to head back to the hospital?"

"I am." Then Selena thanked Meghan again and rode with Peter to the hospital.

"Trevor will be on duty watching over the two of you there tonight. The men who were driving the Mazda left fingerprints in the car. They weren't expecting us to find it like that so they hadn't wiped anything down."

"That's good, more evidence against them."

Peter left Selena off at Daniel's hospital room and headed home. Daniel was sound asleep when she entered the room, and she didn't want to wake him. She climbed onto the couch bed, pulled the sheet and blanket over her, and closed her eyes, but it took her forever to fall asleep while she thought of the danger that Daniel had been in.

"Morning, sweetheart," Daniel said as Selena woke on the couch. "Did you sleep okay?"

"Yeah, sure. What about you? How is your arm?" She sat up on the couch.

"Much better."

"I'm glad for it."

"I'm ordering breakfast. What would you like to have?"

She walked over and sat on his bed to look at the menu with him. "Hmm, the ham, cheese, and vegetable omelet looks good. Orange juice. And that's it."

"I'll have the same thing." Then he filled it out on his chart. "All right. Should be here in about a quarter of an hour." He set the menu on the table.

Then he cuddled with her and they kissed. "I can't wait to go home with you and continue having a good time."

"Me too. I hate the brothers for one of them shooting you and delaying things between us."

"A mating?" He was so hopeful that's what she meant.

"Yes." She smiled.

"Hell, yeah."

She laughed. "We're soulmates, don't you know?"

"Absolutely."

When they finished their breakfast, Peter came by to pick Selena up to take her to the shop. She kissed Daniel goodbye. "See you at lunch."

"Looking forward to it."

Once Selena and Peter arrived at the store, she was busy putting merchandise on the shelves while Peter fielded calls from work. "Yeah, Daniel is all right. I'm certain he would like you to drop by and check on him. No, she's at the shop."

That made her wonder how others would feel about her abandoning Daniel at the hospital.

Then she opened the shop and already had a couple of customers. "Come in. Is there anything you're looking for?"

"Those little skeletons in all the shops. They said you carry them."

She was thrilled that the other ladies were helping her to sell her merchandise by displaying it in their shops.

After the customers bought several items and left the store, Selena called Daniel. "How are you doing?"

"Just lying around, sleeping some. How's the shop going?"

"I've been selling. But I wanted to make sure you are okay."

"The staff is taking good care of me. I'm glad you're at the shop making some sales. I've just been sleeping a lot."

"You're not too lonely, are you?"

"Nah. I'm looking forward to having lunch with you."

"What would you like to have for lunch?"

"A hamburger, fries, and a chocolate milkshake."

She laughed. "You got it. Do you want me to drop by at eleven or twelve?"

"Eleven. I can't wait to see you."

"All right, I'll see you then." She ended the call, glad to be meeting with him soon. "So, Peter, who has the best burgers in town?"

"I make the best ones on the grill at home, but both the tavern and Wolff restaurant have great ones too."

"I guess we'll go to the tavern since it's closer to the hospital."

"I'll call in an order for eleven or twelve?"

"Eleven." She didn't want Daniel to have to wait to eat if he was hungry, and she wanted to be with him. She wondered who had called to see if he was accepting visitors.

"Okay." Peter placed the order. "It will be ready when we are."

"Sounds good." She hung up a clock in the store, then went back to unpacking boxes. But she couldn't stop watching the clock.

"Ready to go?" Peter finally said.

"Yes." She grabbed her bag, locked the door, and headed out with Peter.

They dropped by the tavern, and Peter and Selena went inside to get the food. She was going to run in by herself, but Peter seemed to want to be her shadow even though the tavern allowed only shifters entry.

She paid for the meals, and then she and Peter drove to the hospital.

He went inside with her and checked on Daniel before he left them alone. "Hey, bud, how are you doing?"

"Good. I'm ready to go home."

"Not until the doctor approves that you can go home," Peter said.

Dr. Summerfield dropped by and smiled. "Tomorrow morning. You're healing well, and you'll have to do light duties until your arm heals up more, but you should be good otherwise."

"Thanks, Doc."

"All right, well, your nurse will keep me posted, and I'll check on you later. Keep up the good work." Then Dr. Summerfield left the room.

"I'm going home to have lunch with Meghan. Trevor is on duty in the meantime." Peter said. "I'll come back in an hour to take you back to the shop."

"Okay, sounds good." She put their food on a table and sat next to Daniel on the bed. "I hope you're hungry. This smells delicious."

"I'm hungry. It's just my arm that hurts."

"I hope it feels better soon."

He sat up a bit straighter. "With you being here and the great food, I feel better already."

"Do you want me to stay here and just keep the shop closed for the afternoon?" She took a bite of her burger.

"No. You're selling at the shop, aren't you?"

"Yes. But I don't want you to be bored."

"I'm going to sleep, and I'll see you for dinner. Besides, some of the men have been coming by and bugging me."

Not the women? Single women? That's what she had thought was happening. All the single she-wolves were dropping by to comfort him. She was glad to hear that wasn't so. She realized he handled single men approaching her better than she did, even though she had been thinking that single women would go after Daniel.

Just then, a man walked in the room who looked just like Daniel, surprising her.

"Selena, this is my twin brother, Michael. And, Michael, this is Selena Rivers, the new shopkeeper of the Howling Wolf."

Michael hugged her. "I heard Daniel had laid claim to you as soon as he could."

"You better believe it," Daniel said, sounding proud of himself for doing so.

Selena laughed.

"We'll have you and Carmela over for dinner as soon as we can." Daniel reached for Selena's hand and squeezed in an intimate touch.

"I had to check on you to see how you are doing, but Carmela also wanted me to tell you we'll have you over for dinner. She would have come, but she's still working. She's dying to meet you, Selena. And by the way, she's a distant cousin to Lelandi."

"A red wolf then," Selena said. "That's so cool."

"Yes. She and I were in the army, retired. I'm a Green Beret. Daniel decided to retire to Silver Town after we did also."

"Are you both Green Berets?"

"Yeah," the brothers both said at the same time.

"That's so cool. Okay, well, I'll get out of your hair so you can enjoy your visit. Get better quickly, brother," Michael said.

"Thanks for dropping by," Daniel said.

"Good to meet you," Selena said, thinking that he would be her brother-in-law. She wanted to meet his mate too.

Then Peter called her. "Are you ready to return to the shop?"

She realized then that an hour had already passed. "Yeah, sure." Though she really wanted to stay with Daniel longer.

"Okay, I'm on my way to pick you up."

"See you in a few minutes." Then she ended the call and said to Daniel, "Let me know what you want for dinner, and I'll bring it around six."

"Okay, sounds good. I'll call you before then."

He looked tired, and she figured he would sleep for a while. She kissed him just as Peter arrived. "Rest."

"I will."

Then she left with Peter, but he got a call on Bluetooth. "Yeah, what's up?"

"We had a Blue Ford Mustang stolen, belonging to Mrs. Hastings. We put out a BOLO on it."

"Have the alert roster notified that the brothers who shot Daniel are most likely responsible for the theft of Mrs. Hasting's car. They're armed and dangerous. Do not approach them without backup if you see her car," Peter said.

When he finished the call, Selena asked, "Do you think they'll leave town now?"

"They might. But they may just stay here because they don't think we have the force to apprehend them. Everyone will be looking for them. They don't realize it's not just our sheriff's department, but all of us in Silver Town. They'll get caught."

She didn't know why they would stay in the area though. They'd already threatened her and looked for the file, but hadn't found their father's. So they could still be after that.

"What if I give them the file?" she asked Peter.

"What?"

"The brothers want their dad's file. What if I leave it for them somewhere so they can take the file with them? I've also got it in the Cloud. The information isn't going to help them with their father's case."

"We can't let them go after they'd tried to kill Daniel and after they had transported a couple of skeletons in their vehicle, stolen vehicles, and everything else."

"Of course not. The file will be the bait. If they destroy the files, I have a backup. But they need to be caught and charged with multiple crimes."

"How would we get the word out to them? We've tried tracking their phones, but they must have them turned off." Peter parked in front of her shop.

They both got out of his vehicle, she unlocked the shop, and they went inside.

"Besides, though they're amateurs at all of this, if you were able to tell them you would give them the file, I'm sure they'll suspect it's a setup."

"True. I just wondered if offering to give them the file would be the end of it." Selena put the open sign out for customers. Then she made a sign for the window listing the shop's hours. She would need to have lunch coverage and someone at the shop when she needed to leave for any reason. If she had an active following, she had to have reliable hours.

Peter was in the back of the shop on his phone, coordinating efforts to pursue the three brothers.

Selena called Silva. "Hey, it's me, Selena. Do you know of anyone who could cover my shop when I have to leave?"

"I used a lady named Trish Walker, but she didn't want to work full-time, so I ended up hiring a couple of other ladies. Trish likes part-time jobs, and she's an excellent employee. If she isn't available, post an ad in the paper about what you're looking for. Part-time help?"

"Right. Okay, thanks."

"Brett will help you with an ad if she doesn't work out." Silva gave her Trish's phone number and email address.

Selena got some customers. "Thanks, got to go." They ended the call. "Can I help you with anything?"

"We're just looking to see what you have at the new shop." The woman and her friends looked like they'd been hiking, wearing hiking boots and cargo pants, sweaters and jackets, and must have come into town to shop a bit. They were human, so they were not local.

Then some more customers arrived, same thing, human, probably enjoying the fall scenery around Silver Town and the hiking trails.

"Have you had trouble here?" one of the women asked, pointing toward Peter, wearing his sheriff's uniform.

10

Great. Selena didn't want to explain to customers that the sheriff had to protect her shop because she could be in danger, which meant they could be in peril while they shopped there.

"No trouble," Peter said to the ladies. "I just dropped in to get my wife a gift, and then I got a call I had to handle."

Peter's response was great. He then received another call and began attending to it.

The ladies brought their merchandise to the counter, wiping out more of her fall sweaters.

"I love these. They're so original."

"And long," the one woman said.

Then Selena wrapped up their purchases, and they left. She straightened the shop up, and then Peter was off his phone again. "Thanks for the save," she said.

"You're welcome. I knew you were in a tight spot. With our wolves, everyone knows why we have a police presence here, and they would be fine with it."

"Yeah, but I'm not sure humans would have been!"

"I'M REALLY FINE," Daniel told the doctor when he returned to check on his wound.

"Selena will be staying with you to take care of you?"

"Yes, Doc."

"You're supposed to be protecting her."

"Peter will have someone watching the house," Daniel said.

"You'll rest?"

"Bed rest, couch rest, watch movies, nothing more."

"All right. I'll check with Peter, and you can go home tonight as long as he has the manpower to protect you."

"Thanks, Doc." Daniel resisted the urge to raise his arms and cheer. He could see himself groaning in pain if he lifted his injured arm, and the doctor making him stay there for longer.

"Don't make me regret it."

"I won't, Doc."

As soon as the doctor left the room, Daniel called Selena. "They are releasing me tonight. Peter can drive us home. We can fix dinner and watch movies, if you like."

"That's wonderful. Hang on." She began speaking to someone in the shop.

He was afraid he was interrupting a sale.

Then she got back on the line. "The doctor just spoke to Peter and told him you have bed rest. No lifting with your injured arm. If you feel dizzy or have a fever, you have to go to the hospital right away."

"Yes." However, Doc hadn't mentioned that part to him. He would probably receive the information in the discharge paperwork.

"Peter will have someone watching the house day and night. And I'll fix all our meals. I've hired Trish Walker to run the shop when I'm not there. She worked for Silva before she got full-time employees, and Trish also worked part-time for Maxine. So I'm sure she can cover for me during meals and when I need to be there for you, which will be for the next few days. She'll be thrilled. She wanted more work."

"That's great. I was worried I was interrupting a sale."

"No, but I just got some more sales I need to take care of."

"That's great. I'll see you tonight."

"I'm looking forward to it."

When they ended the call, he felt thrilled that he would be returning home with Selena tonight. The hours wouldn't pass soon enough.

SELENA FINALLY RECEIVED a shipment of black, green, and orange braided wool rugs that gave the appearance that the center of the circle was a hole, and climbing out of the hole was a skeleton, a witch, or a black kitten. They were even prettier than pictured. She took pictures of them, then hung up one of each on either side of the mirror and another on the opposite wall.

Then she emailed all her customers who had signed up to receive notifications when she received new merchandise, sending photos of the rugs. They looked so realistic, she just loved them.

She didn't expect anyone who had recently purchased her merchandise to come back and buy the rugs this soon, but she wanted to share, as she said she would.

Maxine suddenly popped into Selena's shop. "I have to have the black kitten in the rug."

"I just love them. I feel as though I would step right into the hole and fall into it," Selena said.

"Oh, yes, they're so lifelike."

Selena was going to put it in a sack, but Maxine declined the offer.

"I'm taking it straight to the shop and putting it in the entryway."

Selena smiled. "You'll have to let me know how it does."

"I will. See you later." Maxine bounced out of there holding the rug.

Then Laurel called. "Hold one of the skeleton rugs for us. No wait. Meghan said Peter is at the shop watching over you. Tell him to buy one for our store."

Selena laughed. "All right, I will."

When they ended the call, Selena conveyed Laurel's request to Peter.

He smiled and drew out his wallet. "Your merchandise is going to break the bank."

But it was great business for Selena. If anyone liked the rugs in the other shops and asked where they were sold, they would tell them where they were available.

Then Silva rushed into the shop. "I saw Maxine carrying the cat rug out of the store." Then she saw the rugs on display. "Oh, they are beautiful."

"Laurel called to get the skeleton rug for their hotel."

"Okay, I'll get the witch one then. I love all of them. Did you know that the Victorian Era was big on the occult, the paranormal, fortune-telling, seances, and the like? They would have tea parties during Halloween." Silva admired the beautiful rug, running her hand over the soft texture.

"No, I didn't know that." But Selena thought it was fascinating.

"Also, the Wolff family's lodge holds a Halloween party. Everyone comes dressed in costumes. We usually have a theme, but this year it's a free-for-all. It's at seven when all the downtown shops are closed. We dress up in our costumes and offer candy at the shops all day long."

"That sounds like fun."

"It is. Even our tavern is closed so we can go to the party. The Halloween event is wolf-only. Well, for other shifters also in case any show up."

"What are you going as?"

"Pirates with three-cornered hats and swords. Food, drink, and dancing will be the business at hand."

"That sounds great."

"Do you have any idea what you might be?" Silva asked.

"I'll wear a Greek dress and be Princess Andromeda. I had it for a party I went to a couple of years ago. Not a Halloween party, just a themed party."

"Oh, how fun. Well, I've got to get back to the tea shop. Good luck with your new rugs. They look fabulous and so realistic."

"I agree. Enjoy yours."

"Oh, I will. I want to see how many people will avoid stepping on it so they don't fall into the 'hole'." Then Silva took her rug and returned to the tea shop.

Deputy Trevor stopped by the shop, and Selena thought he was going to relieve Peter, but instead, he asked Selena for the rug Laurel wanted. "She wants me to take it over to the hotel."

Peter explained, "Meghan and her sisters wanted it dropped off right away. They didn't want to wait until your shop was closed for the night."

She thought that was cute. She started thinking about Daniel and whether he wanted to wear a costume that matched hers for the Halloween party. She was excited about doing that with him.

She loved to dance, though the guy she'd been with before didn't like to, and it was a chore to get him to the floor for one or two dances. She hoped Daniel liked to dance.

When the shop was quiet, she called Daniel. "Hey, you're not trying to sleep, are you?"

"No, what's up?"

"Silva just told me about the Halloween party."

"Oh, yeah, in two weeks. I forgot to mention it. I planned to take you to the party. Is that all right with you?"

"Sure. I have a Greek dress I was going to wear to the shop that day, then to the party. Do you want to wear something to match? I can be Princess Andromeda, and you are Perseus, my rescuer from the sea monster."

He laughed. "Sounds perfect. I'll have to get a costume for the period, but that should be fun."

"Great. Do you dance?"

"Hell, yeah. When I was on active duty with the Army, we had many dances that we were required to attend. I danced with the single women, though they were human so I never dated any. But I love to dance. What about you?"

"Absolutely. If your arm feels well enough by then." She'd forgotten about that.

"It will. It should be good in a few days."

"I'm excited about the party and dressing up for it."

"Me too. I'm glad Silva mentioned it."

Another woman entered the shop. "I am also. Oh, I have to go. Get some rest."

"I will."

Then they ended the call, and the new customer said, "I'm looking for the rug with a skeleton crawling out of the...oh, there they are. I'm staying at the Silver Town Hotel and I loved theirs." She examined each rug style. "They're all so adorable. I'll take one of the skeleton rugs. I'm going home today and having a Halloween party at my house. It will be perfect for greeting my friends when they arrive."

"That sounds like fun."

Then two more women entered the shop, and one saw the woman holding the rug with the skeleton. "Oh, this is the shop that is carrying those rugs. We saw the one in the dress shop next door with the kitten."

"I'm getting one for my Halloween party at my home," the other woman said, clutching the skeleton rug.

"Oh, it should go over fabulously. I want to get the one with the cat. We're going to the tea shop next door afterward."

"Silva, the owner, has drinks, soups, and sandwiches, and desserts that are out of this world," Selena said.

"That's where I'm going to go too then," the first woman said.

The ladies purchased their rugs and then headed next door to Silva's tea shop.

When they left, Peter said, "You're good for each other's businesses."

"We are. This has been great."

Mainly because the other shops were buying her merchandise, displaying it in their stores, and sharing where they'd purchased it. But it was easy to promote Silva's food and drinks too.

Before her shop closed for the night, Roxie dropped in. "I had to see the new rugs. Oh, my, they're even more colorful and adorable than the pictures indicated. I'll get one of the witches to sit on the floor of our gift shop. How many have you sold?"

"I had ten of each. I sold twenty-eight to humans and wolves."

"I'm not surprised. They're a real conversation piece. I'm glad I got one then. Did Daniel mention the Halloween party at our lodge? We open three banquet rooms for it."

"Silva did."

"Men, typical."

Selena laughed. "We're excited about coming."

"We're thrilled you'll be there. I've got to get back to the lodge. I have to get ready for a wedding ceremony in one of the banquet rooms. We never know how smoothly they'll go."

"Good luck with that."

"Thanks." Then Roxie left the store with her rug.

Selena said, "Yes!"

Peter laughed.

Selena had forgotten he was sitting in the back of the shop, conducting business. "They have a ton of traffic at the lodge's gift shop. It could help with sales."

"I agree."

Selena needed to buy something from the other ladies' shops to help promote their wares. Then she received a box containing little hand-carved howling wolves, some in wood and others in marble. Each was unique, and she set them all about the store.

She wasn't going to send another email notification to all her customers. She didn't want to overwhelm them with too many announcements of new stock deliveries. Besides, this was the Howling Wolf, and they looked great in the shop. She figured some customers might want tokens to remember their visit to Silver Town.

"Time for closing, Peter." But as soon as she said it, a group of five women entered the shop.

They made it worthwhile to stay open for an extra half hour, but she hated to make poor Daniel wait for her.

"I'll let Daniel know we're running late," Peter said.

"Thanks." Selena bagged another two sweaters for one of the ladies.

Another got a black cat T-shirt.

Two of the ladies picked up the last of the braided rugs.

The last one tried on several fall T-shirts, taking forever to decide on one.

Then the ladies left with their purchases, and Selena turned off the main lights, put up the closed sign on the door, and locked the door. Peter and she headed over to the hospital.

"If you need to go to the grocery store or anywhere else, let me know and I'll make sure you have transportation and protection."

"Thanks. I'll have to see what Daniel has on hand for dinner. I'm sure we can make do for tonight."

"All right."

When they reached the hospital, Daniel was dressed and ready to go. Someone had washed his bloodied uniform. She wished she had thought about getting him a change of clothes. But he looked so happy to see her that she realized it hadn't mattered to him. Just leaving the hospital with her had.

He was wearing a sling but walking just fine, like he hadn't experienced any trauma, and she was glad for that.

"Do you need a wheelchair?" the nurse asked.

"No, thanks, I'm fine," Daniel said.

Then they all walked out to Peter's car while Selena read over the discharge papers. "It says you have a non-restrictive diet. What would you like to eat for dinner?"

"We could have something delivered, or I have the fixings for stuffed bell peppers," Daniel said.

"What appeals to you?"

"The stuffed bell peppers."

"I'll make them then."

When they arrived home, Peter carried her bags into the house. "Trevor will provide protection for tonight."

They greeted Trevor and thanked Peter. Then Selena and Daniel locked the door.

Selena went into the kitchen. "Okay on the stuffed bell peppers..."

"Hamburger, tomato sauce, spices, onions, a dab of mustard, a dash of soy sauce, green bell peppers, and shredded extra sharp cheese sprinkled on top and in the bottom of the bell peppers," Daniel said.

"Sounds delightful."

He was trying to show her where everything was, but she asked, "Aren't you supposed to be lying down resting?"

He smiled. "Just trying to help."

She lifted a jar. "Are these the spices?"

"Yeah, when Bertha Hastings, the owner of the B and B, has time, she makes them from the herbs in her garden, and they're perfect for a variety of dishes."

"That's great." Selena spooned some of the spices out. They smelled delightful. "Mashed potatoes and a salad?"

"Both sound good."

"If that's what appeals, that's what we'll have. Okay, I have all the ingredients. Lie down, and I'll have this done in no time."

She finally finished making dinner and set the meal on the table. "Do they have you on antibiotics?"

"Yeah, they do."

"Okay, no alcohol."

"You can have a glass of wine. Don't worry about me."

"Oh, I'm good." She made them glasses of ice water, and they sat down to eat. "Boy, these bell peppers are good. I've never put cheese inside them before, just on top, but I really like it. And I love the seasoning."

"You put it all together just right. It tastes delicious. So you've never said anything about your family."

"I don't have any left. I was an only child, and my parents died in a bad car accident when I was little. The car seat saved me. I had lived with foster parents but moved out when I was a teen."

"I'm sorry to hear that."

"Yeah, living with a human family was hard to do when I wanted to run as a wolf from time to time."

"What made you want to become a forensic anthropologist?"

"Since the time I was a kid, I have loved the study of fossils, including early man. I was fifteen when I was out running as a wolf and came across the skeleton of a murdered man. I wanted so badly to learn who he was. I really wanted to help the police solve crimes. Sometimes we ended up with decades-old skeletons, some of them over 300 years old. I've helped solve many modern cases. Some were cold cases. All were satisfying."

"I bet."

"Just like the cases you have solved, I imagine."

"They have been. Just like the one we're involved in right now, once we solve it."

"I was thinking of giving the file to the brothers."

"What?" Daniel said.

11

Daniel figured Selena meant she would give the file to the men as bait to catch them, but he didn't think they would fall for it.

"The brothers. What if we give them the file and then they think they're free to go?" Selena asked.

"They tried to kill me. They know we're not going to let them go. Not only that, but they had two skeletons in their possession. We don't know whether they had anything to do with the murdered women. But moving the skeletons brings a charge of tampering with evidence and abuse of a corpse, and unlawful transport of human remains across state lines, plus more charges could be made."

"Well, I meant for you and your men to catch them for sure. Not just give them the file and let them go on their merry way."

"I don't want you to get near them."

"All right." Changing the subject, she sighed and said, "I guess we can't run as wolves for a while."

"Not until my arm is healed. Unless it's an emergency."

She took their empty plates into the kitchen, and he joined her and kissed her. But when he began putting the dishes in the dishwasher, she said, "You are supposed to be resting, not helping me."

"I swear I feel fine. A twinge of pain occasionally is all."

"All right, but if you end up back in the hospital, don't tell me I didn't tell you so."

He smiled. "I'll take it easy."

She finished cleaning up the pots and colander, then set them out to dry. "Do you want to watch a movie and then we'll go to bed?"

"Yeah. It's so nice being home."

"It is." Even she had felt that way about staying with Daniel for another night in the hospital. The couch in the room hadn't been half as comfortable as his big bed.

They finally finished the thriller, which helped them get their minds off the shooting, and headed for bed. She assisted him with removing his uniform, then helped him into lounge shorts. Afterward, she dressed in pajamas and joined him in bed. Even though she had planned to give him his space, not wanting to hurt his arm, he seemed to have other ideas when he wrapped his good arm around her.

"Are you sure you're all right sleeping this way?" she asked, snuggling against him, enjoying the heat of his body, the spicy scent of him, his pheromones enticing her own.

"Yeah. If it bothers me in the night, we can cuddle a different way."

She smiled, loving that he wanted to be close to her no matter what. She sure wanted to be close to him tonight. "How are you feeling about the shootout?"

"Annoyed that I didn't take them out."

"I don't blame you. Do you feel any PTSD from getting shot, like during the bank robbery?"

"Yeah. While in the Army, we came under fire on more than one occasion. Your heart pounds, and you're sure you'll get hit under the barrage of bullets. But then you survive the day and you're ready for the next time. But I have to admit that if I'm in another shootout like this, it's going to bother me."

"I feel the same way about being stalked. My heart races and skin chills when I think someone is following me with evil intent."

"I totally understand that." He gave her a squeeze, telling her that he was there for her, which she appreciated.

They moved around a few times so he could get comfortable. The next thing she knew, it was time to get up. She wanted to stay with him like this, enjoying the intimacy between them, but she knew she had to get ready for the shop.

"I've got breakfast." She hugged and kissed him.

He didn't seem to want to let her go either. Then he finally released her, and she hurried out of bed, changed clothes, and walked into the kitchen to make breakfast.

Once she made coffee for them, he came out wearing his pajama bottoms, his arm in a sling, his chest bare. "Sorry. I forgot you might need help dressing," she said, giving him a kiss and a light hug. "You make my day so special."

"You do that for me. As to helping me dress, I'm good. I'll just be lounging around the house today until you return from the shop."

"Good. That's just what you need to do. I think I'll bring home the skeleton skulls tonight and work on reconstructing them, if that's all right with you. I'll fix dinner for us before I start."

"Yeah, sure. So you're also a forensic sculptor. I would love to see the process."

"Okay, good. It'll take a while to make them up since I'm not working on one all day long."

"All right." Then he got a call. "They found Bertha Hasting's car in Trenton, New Jersey."

"No sign of the men?"

"No, but they're searching for them all over the city. Only their fingerprints were found inside the car."

"What was the condition of the car?" Since the Mazda had been in a couple of accidents, she hoped Mrs. Hastings's car was okay. She fixed sausages and scrambled eggs for them.

"No accidents. They didn't leave anything in the car, but their fingerprints. It appeared to the police out there that they had abandoned it in a hurry and hadn't had time to wipe it down."

"That's good. So she can get her car back. Maybe the brothers have given up on us." She'd worried that they would have torn it up like they did the other stolen car. But she figured they'd steal another car now.

"It sounds like it."

Selena was relieved. "We have no more need for security."

"I'm glad for it." He took her in his arms and embraced her, kissing her forehead.

"Me, too. Okay, I'm off to work. You remember to rest." She hugged him warmly, knowing the stars had aligned when they met each other.

He hugged her firmly and kissed her forehead. "Of course. See you for lunch."

Trevor poked his head in. "No more security detail?"

"Not since they found Bertha's car in New Jersey."

"They have it impounded, and we've got a tow truck picking it up," Trevor said. "Peter told me to take Selena to the shop unless you want to loan her your vehicle."

"Sure, she can take my SUV."

For two days, she went to work, had lunch with Daniel, and returned home for dinner. She'd already started driving her own car on the second day. They'd been doing a lot more than cuddling each other at bedtime, but he was still favoring his injured arm. She hoped they would soon be able to do more than that.

This time when she arrived home, everything was different. She saw roses on the dining room table and champagne glasses and was excited to hear the good news.

DANIEL HAD WANTED to make this a special night since he was feeling great. His arm was healed enough, and he wanted to go further with Selena tonight—all the way, if she was ready to mate. He loved her to the moon and back.

He'd dressed in a nice shirt and slacks, then grilled steaks and corn on the cob, started baking potatoes, and made spinach. He even had a chilled bottle of champagne for the occasion. Red roses decorated the table, and he was playing soft music in the background when he heard her drive into the garage.

As soon as she walked inside the house, she smiled at him. "Something smells good. And...you're not wearing your sling."

"No, I'm all good."

"That's for sure. What are we having? Steaks?"

"Yeah, and baked potatoes, spinach, and corn-on-the-cob."

"Roses and champagne? Did they catch the brothers?"

Daniel laughed, figuring she would have gotten the message that this was a special date. "No, unfortunately not. This is more of a romantic liaison."

She chuckled. "Sorry. Of course it is. The roses should have clued me in. They're beautiful and they smell great too. Well, this is so nice."

They ate their dinner and drank their champagne. "Do you want to watch a movie?" he asked.

She set up her materials to reconstruct the first skeleton head, dedicated to learning who the women were. "Nope. I'm not working on reconstructing Jane Doe's face tonight either. We have an important date with destiny."

He pulled her into his arms and rocked her back and forth. "I love you, you know."

"I love you just as much. I was so angry at the brothers for shooting you when we could have mated a couple of days ago. Because I'm not giving you up for anything."

"Hell, I agree." He grabbed her hand and headed to the bedroom, where they would become mated wolves. "I couldn't imagine being with anyone else."

"I know. Me either. And it was so nice coming home to a delightful meal, champagne, and roses."

"I always want to be there for you like that."

"I want the same for you."

When they reached the bedroom, he was ready to rip off his clothes.

For a heartbeat, they stood in the hush, eyes sharpening, hearts drumming in tandem, the future rushing up to meet them: fall's vivid colors beyond the window, the sweat-laced heat already rising between their bodies. He made as if to peel off his clothes at once, hands eager at the hem of his shirt, but she intercepted him midmotion, her own hands reaching for his collar, intent on slowing the tempo, savoring the moment.

She undid the top button—then the next, and the next—her knuckles grazing his collarbone, the warmth of her hands painting new directions over his skin. Instead of rushing headlong, she traced the muscles of his chest.

Her touch sent his pheromones spiraling, and hers drove him crazy.

She parted his shirt and pressed her lips to his skin, leaving slow, deliberate kisses that anchored him to the moment, to the reality of her. The urgency in him was pronounced, but her slow touch made him appreciate her even more.

He surrendered to her rhythm, framing her face between his hands and kissing her lips, the corners of her mouth, her jawline, before speaking against the softness of her cheek, "You are just the one for me."

Her answer came low and sure. "And you are that for me." The sentence was a contract in the certainty of her touch and words.

He corralled her against him, and now it was his turn to undress her, his hands working beneath her burgundy sweater, fingers trailing fire along her ribs as he lifted the wool up and over her head. The sweater fell to the carpet. He let his shirt follow, not minding where it landed, only that it was gone.

Now her skirt—heavy, pleated wool—was the last significant barrier, and he thumbed open the buttons at her waist, peeling it off so it puddled in a soft heap. She stepped out of it as if shedding a skin, meeting his gaze with a wolf's confidence.

She unfastened his belt with a practiced deftness, and she undid the fly of his jeans, hands pressing against him through the fabric, teasing at the threshold. He kicked off his shoes with one foot, the pair tumbling askew under the bed. She followed suit, unzipping her boots, removing them and her socks, her bare toes flexing against the soft rug.

He pulled off his pants and dropped them on the growing pile of clothes. After removing her lavender bra, freeing her breasts, her dusky nipples already aroused, he slipped her matching pair of panties off. She did the honors of removing his boxer briefs, and his dick was already at full mast, revealing just how eager he was to make love to her.

He swept her up along the side of the bed, catching her in a half-dip, one arm curled behind her knees. She kept her eyes on him, never darting away, even as his hands mapped the length of her body, learning the territory anew. They clung together, skin to skin, the heat between them building until it seemed the room itself must combust.

He swept her hair aside to kiss her neck, while she stroked his back in long, reverent arcs. He pressed himself against her, and she arched up to meet him, their legs tangling, their arms entwined.

He began stroking her between the legs, breathing in their

pheromones, loving that they were so in harmony with one another.

She writhed against his fingers, moaning in the grip of orgasm, and howled when she came.

He laughed. "Are you ready?" Because when he entered her, they would be mated wolves, and it couldn't be undone.

"Yes, for sure. Do it."

He was glad she didn't want to put it off because he was so ready for this. He entered her and began to thrust into her tight body. She felt so good, and just where he belonged. She was scraping her long nails against his back in a gentle caress at the same time. He pumped into her until he felt the coming explosion. Bathing her with his hot seed, he lay on top of her in a state of bliss.

Then he rolled over and tugged her on top of him, naked skin to naked skin. "You feel so good. I love you, honey."

"You are my wolf forever and ever. I love you so much."

THE NEXT DAY, excited about the mating, they told everyone they were mated wolves, thrilling the pack members. They had dinner with his brother, Michael, and his mate, Carmela, that evening.

The brothers grilled chicken thighs and vegetables, while the ladies made cocktails and potato salad.

"We're so glad Daniel was able to connect with you. When Michael and I met, Daniel and my brother were going to make sure we were a good fit for a mating. We mated before they could interfere."

Selena laughed, finished boiling the eggs, and placed them in a bowl of ice water to cool them down and remove the shells. "We were ready to mate. No one would have told us what to do."

"For sure. Now if we'd just been humans, that would have been a different story. But with our wolf genetics, we know when it's right for us. So Daniel said you're reconstructing the faces of the unknown women who had been shot."

"Yes. I'm nearly done with the one. I was working on it at the shop when I didn't have customers."

"Did anyone catch you at it?"

She smiled. "A few. They were fascinated, thankfully. Most of the time, I would put it behind the counter, but a couple of times, I didn't hide it fast enough. As soon as I finish it up, I'll take pictures of her, and I'll share them with law enforcement agencies. I was thinking they might not have been from Fort Wayne, Indiana, like I thought. They might have been passing through. Or killed somewhere else entirely."

Carmela frowned. "I sure hope it gets resolved quickly. The women need justice, and their families need to be notified."

"I agree."

"No word about finding the brothers in Trenton, I take it."

"None. No telling where they are now."

Carmela began adding the cooked and cut-up potatoes to a bowl. Selena finished peeling the eggs and added them to the bowl.

Carmela added sliced up pickles, mayonnaise, and a little mustard. "You're going to the Halloween party at the Timberline Ski Lodge, aren't you?"

"Yes, as a Greek mythology couple."

"Oh, how fun. Michael and I haven't decided on what to wear. Would you mind if we joined you in the Greek garb?"

"Oh, no, that would be fun. We could sit at the same table and represent it together." Since they were family now, Selena thought it could be cute.

"That would be great."

Then they finished making the potato salad and took the drinks out to the men.

"We're going as Greek mythology partygoers since Selena and

Daniel are wearing those kinds of clothes." Carmela took a sip of her drink.

"I'm finally glad we decided on something," Michael said.

"I've been waffling about it for weeks," Carmela said. "I knew Michael would be glad that we have decided on something."

Even though Carmela had done all the deciding, Selena mused.

When they sat down to eat in the dining room, Michael toasted to the new couple.

"Oh, what about a wedding?" Carmela asked.

"I want to do it before Halloween," Daniel said.

"Not a Halloween wedding?" Carmela asked.

"No, right before. That should give us time if we can reserve a banquet hall at the Timberline Ski Lodge."

"Everyone will want to come," Carmela said. "You might need the three banquet halls."

Selena got on her phone and asked Roxie, "Can we reserve a banquet room for a wedding before Halloween?"

"You'll need all three banquet rooms because the turnout for the pack is phenomenal for celebrations like this. The first time we could book all three rooms is December 15th, and only because we had a cancellation. The bride and groom had a falling out."

"Oh, no, that's terrible. But good for us. Will December 15th be all right with you, Daniel?" Selena asked him.

"Yeah, sure."

"That will give everyone more time to prepare for it," Roxie said.

"All right. I want you and Kayla, Silva, the MacTire sisters, and Carmela to be my matrons of honor, and Maxine to be a bridesmaid."

"I'm honored," Roxie said. "Kayla will be thrilled. We'll assist you with anything you need help with."

"That would be terrific," Selena said, then they ended the call.

"Let me know what I can help with, and thanks for choosing me, too," Carmela said.

Knowing Daniel, he had wanted to avoid a long-drawn-out affair of planning for the wedding. But Roxie was right. They needed some time to plan for everything.

After a lovely celebratory dinner and chocolate cheesecake for dessert, they said their goodnights and headed home.

"Michael gave me a hard time for not giving him a heads-up so he could approve a mating between us," Daniel said.

"Because you wanted to approve his mating to Carmela."

Daniel smiled. "Yeah. I hadn't even met her yet. At least Michael had met you before we mated."

"Nothing would have changed between your brother and Carmela if you'd had a say in it."

Daniel chuckled. "Yeah, you're right."

"Do you want to watch a movie while I finish sculpting Jane Doe #1?"

"That would be fine."

"I'm just so close to finishing it, I would like to get her picture out to law enforcement."

"And then start on the other."

"Yes. It may be a case where the women were connected or not, but perhaps one or both will appear on a missing persons list." She began working at the table while watching TV with Daniel. When she was done, she took the photos and then sent them to law enforcement. Once that was finished, she curled up with Daniel on the sofa to watch the rest of the movie.

When the movie ended, he whipped her up in his arms and carried her to bed. "This calls for another celebration."

12

A few days later, Daniel dropped by Selena's shop to pick her up for the Halloween party.

"It's time to party." She pirouetted, showing off her gold-trimmed, gold-belted white Grecian dress.

Wearing a short tunic and a short burgundy cloak, he took her in his arms and whirled her around. "You are beautiful. I can't wait to dance with you."

"Ditto. And you are so sexy. I just love you in this." She ran her hand over his wool tunic.

Then they left the shop, locked it up, and climbed into Daniel's SUV.

"So how are the wedding plans coming along?" Daniel had left it up to the ladies, though they asked his input on what he wanted to wear. Since it was near Christmas, he wanted to wear a black tuxedo, while the ladies wore red gowns and little white faux-fur capes, and his sweet bride would wear a white gown with a long train. That's all she would reveal.

Daniel's and Carmela's brothers would be his groomsmen, along with Peter and the rest of the deputy sheriffs.

Everyone was excited about going to the wedding.

But for now, it was time to join everyone heading to the Halloween party. "How was your day?" he asked, hoping Selena's sales would continue to be good.

"I had fun giving out candy at the shop. I had a lot of sales too, but seeing all the little ones, teens, and some adults all dressed up was great. How about at the sheriff's office?"

"We had several kids dropping by. We gave chocolate out."

She laughed. "I have a mixture of candy."

"We had fun too."

When Selena and Daniel arrived at the banquet hall for the party, a couple of pack members stood at the banquet door, making sure that no one entered who wasn't a wolf—humans looking to crash the party for free food, drinks, and entertainment.

Dance music was playing, and Selena and Daniel met up with Carmela and Michael on the dance floor, happily dancing to the various tunes.

Several others got into the spirit of the music and joined them, no matter what they were wearing.

Darien Silver was a gladiator, and his mate, Lelandi, was a redheaded Cleopatra. Wizards, witches, cowboys and cowgirls, astronauts, pirates, you name it, were kicking up their heels and having a blast.

After several dances, the Hoffman family and Silva and Sam sat down at a table together to eat sliced roast beef and grilled veggies. Deviled spider eggs were popular—little black olives cut in strips on top that made them like spiders. And all kinds of desserts were made up in Halloween fashion—cookies trimmed with icing spiders, chocolate witches' hats, mini-ghost cakes, and an assortment of other festive treats.

"Love your pirate costumes," Selena said to Sam and Silva.

"Thanks, sugar." Selena removed her three-cornered hat. "We're still looking for the treasure."

Sam laughed. "I found mine." He leaned over and kissed her.

"Now that is just the right thing to say," Carmela said.

"We love your Grecian costumes. Very sexy," Silva said.

"Thanks. This has been so much fun," Selena said. "I've never been to a Halloween party before and didn't know what to expect."

"They're enjoyable. All the celebrations here are. Everyone does their own thing for Christmas. They have private parties. But we do have a Christmas parade with Santa and Mrs. Claus. They have a New Year's Eve and Valentine's Day party at the banquet hall. The Fourth of July party and Easter parties are at the pack leaders' home. They used to have a Thanksgiving celebration there, but then the pack got too big. So everybody does their own thing," Silva said.

"So there are lots of celebrations to enjoy," Sam said. "We also have Victorian Days where we all dress up for that."

"Oh, how fun. This sounds like a great place to live for adults and children alike. A great place to raise children," Selena said.

Silva and Sam both smiled at her.

"In the future, I mean, about the kids," Selena said, laughing.

Everyone laughed.

"We thought you had some news for us," Carmela said.

"Not this soon," Selena said.

Daniel squeezed her hand and smiled.

They finished their dinner and then all of them got up to dance. They only stopped long enough to get drinks of water, and then they were up dancing again.

They stayed until the bewitching hour, and then everyone said good night to everyone else. On the way home, Daniel took hold of Selena's hand and kissed it. "You are the perfect dance partner."

"I feel the same way about you. I'm signing us up for all the dances."

He laughed. "I'm ready for them. I haven't danced that much in one night ever. But being with my mate, I had the best time ever."

"I haven't danced that much at one event either. It was great. We also have our wedding coming up. I guess we won't be doing a lot of dancing at that though."

"We'll make up for it at the other dances," he said.

"I know why I mated you." She smiled. "My dance partner for life. At the Halloween party, the costumes were all so great."

"Ours were the best."

She agreed. "We did get a ton of flattering remarks, and we complimented each other. On another subject, tomorrow night, I'll finish up Jane Doe number two's facial reconstruction, take the pictures, and send them off. I can't believe the other one didn't get any hits."

"I know, but family and friends might not have reported her as missing." He parked in the garage, closed the garage door, and they went inside the house.

But instantly, they smelled that the three brothers had been there, and neither Selena nor Daniel had their guns with them since they had been at the Halloween party.

Plus, they really had thought the brothers were long gone.

He didn't see the men, who might be hiding in the house, waiting for them to return.

He motioned for Selena to stop and return to the garage. She stepped backward into the garage and began texting on her phone. Daniel saw that the second Jane Doe's partial reconstruction, which had been sitting on the dining room table, was no longer there.

He wanted to get his gun from the gun safe, but it was in the bedroom. It was impossible to tell where the men were. He suspected that they were hiding in the house and hadn't left. Were they in the bedroom?

He suspected they were. Anticipating ambushing them. Had they heard the garage door rumble as it opened? He wasn't sure. He could hear it, being a wolf, but the master bedroom was on the other side of the house, so humans might not be able to hear it.

Still, he thought that if they tried to open the garage door again, they could be rushed, and he didn't have bulletproof car windows. Under a barrage of bullets, Selena and he could be killed.

"Peter and the other deputies are coming," she whispered to Daniel. "Can you move back into the garage and shut the door and lock it?"

"Yeah, but they can unlock it from the other side."

"You can't just stand in the house. Come on back to the garage."

Then he remembered his other gun. "Hell, I've got a gun in the glove box. I was going to put it away before the party, but forgot."

"You still can't shoot it out with the brothers."

Thinking of the last time he had faced the three men, guns firing, and got shot, he had to agree. He stepped back into the garage and slowly closed the door.

"I'm turning into my wolf. At least I'll have teeth to fight with." Selena began stripping off her clothes.

"I'm getting my gun out of the glovebox." He locked the garage door with his key. Then he retrieved his gun from the car while Selena finished removing her clothes and shifted into her wolf.

Someone on the other side of the garage door unlocked it. Daniel hit the garage door opener in anticipation of the reinforcements' arrival. But Peter and the others were already too late.

The menaces were coming through the door.

The brothers charged into the garage, guns blazing. Daniel dove down behind his car, his heart pounding. All he worried about was Selena being hit. Selena sneaked around the SUV and leapt on the man closest to her. Daniel shot from under the SUV at the other two brothers in the legs to incapacitate them.

They dropped to the floor, crying out in pain. Selena had made the third guy drop his weapon while she kept hold of his arm, protected by the leather jacket, growling and snarling, putting the fear of the devil in him.

"Get it off me!" the man called out.

Just then, Peter arrived with five other deputies, their lights off and sirens silent.

"Two are down, leg wounds," Daniel said. "My wolf has still got hold of the other one. The man will need to be checked over for bite marks." They couldn't afford to have him bitten and turned, but Daniel suspected that's why Selena had attacked his arm, covered in a leather jacket, forcing him to drop his weapon, but not biting through the heavy material.

Trevor gathered their guns while the EMTs arrived and came to take care of the wounded brothers.

Peter talked to Selena. "You can let him go now. We've got his gun. We need to check him over and take him into custody."

She finally released the third brother, and he put his hands up in the air, his jacket sleeve torn, but Daniel didn't see or smell any blood.

While the wounded men were loaded up in two ambulances, Peter removed the other brother's leather jacket and pulled up his sleeve. No sign of any blood or bite marks. "Looks good."

"Your dog tore up my jacket."

"You're lucky she held back. She has the bite of a wolf and could have chewed your arm right off. She's trained to take down armed combatants. If Daniel had given the word, she would have ripped out your throat." Peter took him in his car. "Meet me down at the station for witness statements," he said to Daniel.

"We'll be there in a minute." He thought about how proud he was of her. Both their hearts were still beating like crazy, and he thanked God that neither of them had been hit by all the rounds the brothers had fired. He closed the garage door so she could shift in privacy.

"I'm going to see how the brothers got into the house." Then he hurried into the house while she quickly shifted and began dressing.

The breeze was blowing into the guest room where one of the

large windows was broken. Bastards. He would have to replace it tomorrow. He also found the nearly finished skull of the second Jane Doe on the guest bed. He was glad that they hadn't broken it and it wouldn't take too long for Selena to finish it.

Selena joined him in the guest room. "Oh, they broke the window. What rotten brothers."

"Yeah, I agree."

But then she lovingly picked up the skull she had been working on. "You're safe. I was worried about you." Then she said to Daniel, "It's a good thing the brother I bit had a heavy jacket on, otherwise I would have had to have shoved the brother down and hope it would have knocked him out. You couldn't take out three at once."

"Yeah, I needed you."

She put Jane Doe's skull back on the bed. "We needed each other." Her heart was still pounding as she pulled him into an embrace. "Let's get the statements done. So we can finish off the Halloween night in the way we had intended."

He smiled at her as he hugged her tightly. "Let's call our statements in."

"Even better."

EPILOGUE

After saying "I do" at their wedding in the banquet halls at the ski lodge, Selena and Daniel kissed. Everyone in the pack had shown up for the wedding and cheered. In a week, she and Daniel were going on their honeymoon to Alaska. But for now, they were going to dance and have dinner with their guests.

They'd had a lovely turkey dinner for Thanksgiving with Daniel's brother and sister-in-law a couple of weeks before.

When they sat down to eat after the wedding ceremony, Peter stopped by their table and said, "Congratulations, you two. We have some news about the Jane Does. They were both identified as former lovers of the brothers' father. He killed them both."

She was glad they'd found the nearly reconstructed head of the second skull in the guest bedroom. She figured the brothers were going to take it with them and bury or destroy it, so she was relieved they hadn't. She was able to finish it up, take the pictures, and send them to law enforcement.

"Oh, wow. I'm glad they were identified and that the murderer was too," Selena said. "I guess the reason the brothers went after Daniel was because he was about to discover the other skeleton in the trunk of their stolen car and have the car confiscated. Then, when they didn't kill him the first time, they came after him to finish the job so he wouldn't be a witness to the shooting."

Daniel raised his brows at Peter. "Now? At the wedding?"

Peter smiled. "I knew Selena would want to know right away that the women had been identified."

"I did. Thanks, Peter."

Meghan came over and took hold of Peter's arm. "I told you to wait to tell them." She smiled at them. "Congratulations, by the way. I'm glad Peter had Daniel approve your business in town."

"Meghan twisted my arm," Peter said, laughing.

Meghan and her sisters had all been into matchmaking, as they had suspected.

"Selena wanted to know about the Jane Does she had worked so hard to reconstruct," Peter said, getting back to the subject at hand.

"Okay, now that she knows, it's time for her to enjoy her wedding celebration. We'll talk later." Meghan dragged Peter away to dance. "Thank you for getting them together."

"It's a good thing it worked out the way you ladies wanted."

Selena sighed. "I'm glad to know that the murdered women's families could be notified, and they already have the murderer behind bars."

"Yeah, me too. I'm glad to get some resolution. And I'm glad the brothers are in jail for attempting to murder me, moving the skeletons with an attempt to get rid of them, and threatening you until their trial comes up."

"I'm really glad that I didn't turn the one brother and that they're in jail. On another topic that's a lot more pleasant, I still can't believe you booked an Alaskan hiking tour out of White Bear with polar bear shifters who have some shifter-only tours, not that anyone would know they're shifters but us."

"Yeah, and that we can actually run as wolves when we're out in the wilderness. They'd heard we were a wolf-shifter-run town, so they were waffling about what kind of a tour we might like, but since we live here, you own a shop, and I'm a deputy sheriff, they asked me if we liked howling at the moon. I had no idea what they were."

She laughed. "That must have been an interesting conversation."

"It was. They said that, for the most part, polar bears were the good guys. So I put two and two together—White Bear is a town run by polar bears. That's when they mentioned they had wild animal tours, and I verified they meant shifters, and they confirmed it. I told them to sign us up, and we're just newly married. They were delighted.

"They've booked rooms for us at waypoints and at the cabins for a newly married/mated couple. Bottles of champagne will be served. Though they said that their guests would share in the celebration. And they'll be in secluded areas where we can run in our animal halves."

"That will be so much fun."

Darien and Lelandi dropped by their table. "We heard you're going on a shifter-run excursion for your honeymoon. Let us know how it goes. We're thinking of taking an anniversary trip up there."

Selena took hold of Daniel's hand. "We sure will."

Silva and Sam came by to congratulate them and discuss their honeymoon trip. It was the latest topic of conversation. "You'll need to let us all know what it's like. We're dying to learn what kind of shifters are on the tour, and to see polar bears up close that aren't going to eat you. That should be a great experience," Silva said.

"That's what we can't wait for. But first, we're going to enjoy the New Year's Eve party," Darien said.

"And lots of dancing." Selena sipped some of her champagne.

"And food and drink," Silva said. "Oh, and I heard you got some cute things in for New Year's Eve. I can't wait to see them in person."

Selena thought her shop would slow down on sales, but it was still hopping. Daniel was still helping her research graveyards at night, and they had a memorial for Wolf McKennick, the first old skeleton she had found, burying him in the cemetery near his brother.

They were running as wolves nightly and finishing off the evenings with a whole lot of loving.

She had never imagined that Daniel's approval of her shop would lead to a mating and a whole new lifestyle. Forget living in an apartment or buying a home of her own. His home was just perfect for the two of them. He was perfect for her.

Daniel was grateful for Meghan and her sisters and their matchmaking. If Meghan hadn't encouraged Peter to give him the assignment to approve Selena's store startup, one of the mated deputies would have done it. Daniel might not have seen her until she was already dating another wolf. Daniel and Selena had all the chemistry in the world. He didn't really believe anyone else would have been a perfect match for her. But it might have taken him longer to get her attention.

She leaned over and kissed him. "A wolf run after the celebration is over?"

"No trip to the cemetery tonight?"

She laughed. "Nope, bedtime play instead."

"I'm all for that! And playing as wolves." But he would always be there for her cemetery visits too.

ACKNOWLEDGMENTS

To Donna Fournier and Darla Taylor, whose eagle eyes caught what mine missed and whose gentle guidance steered me back to clarity. This book stands stronger because of your dedication.

ABOUT THE AUTHOR

USA Today bestselling and award-winning author **Terry Spear** has written over a hundred paranormal romance novels, young adult, and medieval Highland historical romances. Her first werewolf romance, *Heart of the Wolf,* was named a 2008 *Publishers Weekly*'s Best Book of the Year, and her subsequent titles have garnered high praise and hit the *USA Today* bestseller list. A retired officer of the U.S. Army Reserves, Terry lives in Spring, Texas, where she is working on her next werewolf romance, shapeshifting jaguars, cougar shifters, vampires, hot Highlanders, and having fun with her young adult fae and vampire novels, helping with her grand-children and raising two Havanese.

For more information, please visit her website at: http://www.terryspear.com

Blog: https://terryspearbooks.blog/

Follow her for new releases and book deals: www.bookbub.com/authors/terry-spear

Twitter: @TerrySpear.

Facebook: http://www.facebook.com/terry.spear

ALSO BY TERRY SPEAR

Adult Titles

Romantic Suspense: Deadly Fortunes, In the Dead of the Night, Relative Danger, Bound by Danger

***

The Highlanders Series: His Wild Highland Lass (novella), Vexing the Highlander (novella), Winning the Highlander's Heart, The Accidental Highland Hero, Highland Rake, Taming the Wild Highlander, The Highlander, Her Highland Hero, The Viking's Highland Lass, My Highlander, Stolen Highland Dreams

Other historical romances: Lady Caroline & the Egotistical Earl, A Ghost of a Chance at Love

***

Heart of the Wolf Series: Heart of the Wolf, Destiny of the Wolf, To Tempt the Wolf, Legend of the White Wolf, Seduced by the Wolf, Wolf Fever, Heart of the Highland Wolf, Dreaming of the Wolf, A SEAL in Wolf's Clothing, A Howl for a Highlander, A Highland Werewolf Wedding, A SEAL Wolf Christmas, Silence of the Wolf, Hero of a Highland Wolf, A Highland Wolf Christmas; SEAL Wolf Hunting; A Silver Wolf Christmas, SEAL Wolf in Too Deep, Alpha Wolf Need Not Apply, Between a Wolf and a Hard Place, SEAL Wolf Undercover, Dreaming of a White Wolf Christmas, Flight of the White Wolf, All's Fair in Love and Wolf, A Billionaire Wolf for Christmas, SEAL Wolf Surrender, Silver Town Wolf: Home for the Holidays, Night of the Billionaire Wolf, You Had Me at Wolf, Joy to the Wolves, The Wolf Wore Plaid, Jingle Bell Wolf, The Best of Both Wolves, While the Wolf's Away, Christmas Wolf Surprise, Wolf Takes the Lead, Wolf on the Wild Side, Her Wolf for the Holidays, A Good Wolf is

Hard to Find (2024), Dreaming of a Highland Wolf (2024), Wolf Bound, Mated for Christmas (2024) , The Wolf of My Eye

SEAL Wolves: To Tempt the Wolf, A SEAL in Wolf's Clothing, A SEAL Wolf Christmas; SEAL Wolf Hunting, A SEAL Wolf in Too Deep, SEAL Wolf Undercover, SEAL Wolf Surrender

Silver Town Wolves: Destiny of the Wolf, Wolf Fever, Dreaming of the Wolf, Silence of the Wolf; A Silver Wolf Christmas, Between a Wolf and a Hard Place, Home for the Holidays, Jingle Bell Wolf

Wolff Family Lodge Wolves: You Had Me at Wolf, Wolf on the Wild Side, A Good Wolf is Hard to Find

Highland Wolves: Heart of the Highland Wolf, A Howl for a Highlander, A Highland Werewolf Wedding, Hero of a Highland Wolf, A Highland Wolf Christmas, The Wolf Wore Plaid, Her Wolf for the Holidays, Dreaming of a Highland Wolf, The Wolf of My Eye

Billionaire Wolf Series: A Billionaire in Wolf's Clothing, A Billionaire Wolf for Christmas, Night of the Billionaire Wolf, Wolf Takes the Lead

White Wolf Series: Legend of the White Wolf, Dreaming of a White Wolf Christmas, Flight of the White Wolf, While the Wolf's Away, Mated for Christmas

Red Wolf Series: Seduced by the Wolf, Joy to the Wolves, The Best of Both Wolves, Christmas Wolf Surprise

Greystoke Wolf Pack: Wolf Bound,

Wolf Novellas: Day of the Wolf, Seal Wolf Pursuit, Wolf to the Rescue, Night of the Wolf, United Shifter Force, Wolfish

***

Heart of the Jaguar Series: Savage Hunger, Jaguar Fever, Jaguar Hunt, Jaguar Pride, A Very Jaguar Christmas, You Had Me at Jaguar, The Witch and the Jaguar, Dawn of the Jaguar

***

Heart of the Cougar Series: Cougar's Mate, Call of the Cougar, Taming the Wild Cougar, Covert Cougar Christmas, a novella, Double Cougar Trouble, Cougar Undercover, Cougar Magic, Cougar Halloween Mischief, Falling for the Cougar, Cougar Christmas Calamity, Catch the Cougar (Halloween Novella), You Had Me at Cougar, Saving the White Cougar, Big Cat Magic

***

White Bear Series: Loving the White Bear, Claiming the White Bear, Bear of a Halloween, Protecting the White Bear

Grizzly Bear Series: Bear in Mind

***

Highland Wolves of Old: Wolf Pack, Wolf Alliance, Wolf Heir

Heart of the Huntress Series: Killing the Bloodlust, Deadly Liaisons, Huntress for Hire, Forbidden Love, Deadly Liaisons, Vampire Redemption, Primal Desire, Huntress Unleashed

Vampire Novellas: The Siren's Lure, Vampiric Calling, Seducing the Huntress

***

Comedy Romance: Exchanging Grooms, Marriage, Las Vegas Style

***

Science Fiction: Galaxy Warrior

Young Adult Titles

The World of Fae:

The Dark Fae

The Deadly Fae

The Winged Fae

The Ancient Fae

Dragon Fae

Hawk Fae

Phantom Fae

Golden Fae

Falcon Fae

Woodland Fae

Angel Fae

***

The World of Elf:

The Shadow Elf

The Darkland Elf

Warrior Elf

***

Blood Moon Series:

Kiss of the Vampire

Bite of the Vampire

Night of the Vampire

The Vampire Chronicles Series:

The Vampire in My Dreams

Demon Guardian Series:

The Trouble with Demons

Demon Trouble, Too

Demon Hunter

Non-Series for Now:

Ghostly Liaisons

The Beast Within

Courtly Masquerade

Deidre's Secret

The Magic of Inherian:

The Scepter of Salvation

The Mage of Monrovia

Emerald Isle of Mists

Tashama